LOOKING GLASS EDITOR

By

G G Collins

CHAMISA CANYON
PUBLISHING

Chamisa Canyon Publishing
chamisacanyon@live.com
Attn: Rights & Permissions

Book Cover & Interior by Vila Design

Editing by Jay Terre

ISBN 978-1-7354282-1-5

ISBN 978-0-9884674-5-3 (ebook)

Books by G G Collins

Reluctant Medium

Lemurian Medium

Atomic Medium

Anasazi Medium

Presence: A Rachel Blackstone Paranormal Mystery Short Story

Dead Editor File

Looking Glass Editor

Murder USA: A Crime Fiction Tour of the Nation (Contributor)

Flying Change

Without Notice

Forthcoming:

Editor Kill Fee

Skinwalker Medium

AUTHOR'S NOTE

Publishing is a complex industry, at once creative and yet a business. The myriad of details that must be accomplished before a book can be published is difficult to comprehend, especially to the author waiting in the wings.

On average, an author will spend several months to a year writing a book. Whether traditionally or indie published, there are many decisions along the way: white or cream paper, gloss or matte cover, font choice and cover art. Marketing includes sales rep presentation, ARC (advance review copy; also referred to as a galley), choosing reviewers and requesting interviews. And then, there is the yearly trek to BookExpo America for four days, presented by the American Booksellers Association (pre-pandemic). Steps to publication include editing, typesetting, blueline, proofs and finally a book you can hold in your hands. It can take a year to publication unless the publisher fast tracks it because it's topical or urgent reading.

Daily life at a book publisher can range from deadly quiet to abject chaos, all the while processing the hundreds to thousands of manuscripts and queries that arrive daily. Today, more queries are submitted via email, but some writers still use the mail route. Envelopes and boxes holding the blood, sweat and tears of writers are stacked on desks, office floors, hallways and in closets. Most are returned unread by unpaid interns with a form letter and are never seen by editors.

Writers write because they must; because they have stories to tell. Make an author's day and write a short review describing why you liked—or loved their book. The next time you pick up a book, know it was a very long journey to your hands.

ACKNOWLEDGEMENTS & GRATITUDE

My thanks to my lifemate who has acted as my first reader for years and continues to brainstorm with me over dinner and drinks while I'm writing down ideas as fast as I can hoping my dinner doesn't get cold.

Much appreciation to my friends who support and encourage me: Cheryl, Judi and Marilyn.

To Santa Fe, New Mexico, a city rich in history and three cultures, for providing a beautiful and intriguing background. And to Sedona, Arizona and its mysterious red rocks and mystical atmosphere.

Del Charro Saloon is a real restaurant in Santa Fe, found in the Inn of the Governors. It is popular with both visitors and locals. Located on the corner of West Alameda and Don Gaspar, you can watch the world go by or catch the score while enjoying food and margaritas. Pssst. Their green chile is wonderful!

For Cheryl K
My deepest appreciation.

"Books are not seldom talismans and spells."

– William Cowper, British Poet

CHAPTER 1

"Get back," the terrified woman pleaded.

"Who's going to make me?" her ex-husband said coldly as he advanced across the floor of the parking garage. He held a filet knife in his hand. The curved blade gleamed surrealistically in the bare fluorescent light from overhead.

"You can't be here. I have a protective order." The young woman struggled to unlock her car, but her hands shook so badly she dropped the keys in a puddle at her feet.

"Protective order! Big deal. Do you see anyone around to enforce it? The attendant is downstairs. Even if he heard you scream he couldn't get here in time to make any difference."

He was in no hurry. Each step he took was meticulously placed. He would enjoy this. This moment had taken months of searching. He'd followed her from state to state, figured out each new disguise, found her even when she took jobs far beneath her qualifications. He knew what she was thinking before she fully formed the idea herself. She would never deny him anything again. She would never speak another word with that pretty mouth.

Her hands were slippery with water and oil when she fished the keys from the pool of water. By the time she was standing again he was only a few feet away, an easy leap. Even with the keys, she couldn't open the car before he reached her. Was this it? Twenty-seven years was all she would have?

She looked at the man she had married two years ago. Two years wasn't a long time, yet it seemed an eternity. Her love had turned to fear and hatred a few months after their marriage. The beatings, the apologies and finally the court appearances—with a different judge every time—had exhausted her. No one seemed to understand or care when she told them he was going to kill her; no one, except her lawyer. She had implored the court to provide for her safety, but the police couldn't stop him until he actually harmed her. What kind of system gave the criminal more rights than the victim?

When she fled Oregon to supposed safety in Kentucky, he pursued and continued to threaten her. She went through the court scene again and again. One night, with only the clothes she was wearing she ran for her life to New Mexico. Soon the harassment began anew. She considered moving again, and gave notice at the hotel where she worked, but it was too late.

"Come here," he said reaching for her arm.

There was nothing she could do. She no longer felt afraid. Her only feeling was one of resignation. Perhaps she'd been preparing subconsciously for this moment. When she looked into his eyes she saw that gentle man from a wedding not so long ago. He had a dark handsome face and laughing brown eyes. It had been a warm April day. The dogwoods bloomed.

Her mother wept softly throughout the backyard ceremony. Makeup carefully hid the bruise near one eye. She would not be like her mother. Her marriage would be full of love.

He was close enough she could feel his breath on her face.

"I love you," she said.

*　　　*　　　*

Taylor Browning left the early 1930s ornately styled Lensic Performing Arts Center with friend and coworker, Jim Wells. It was a cool evening in Santa Fe and Taylor pulled at her coat but didn't bother to button it. She liked the cold.

"Won't be long now," Jim said rubbing his hands briskly.

"For what?" She hated to ask as it might be a setup. Jim was known around the office for his corrosive, yet witty, personality.

"Skiing of course. Surely you've noticed the runs are white, Taylor dear." He nudged her gently and his eyes twinkled mischievously.

She was a beginning skier at best, and petrified of the lifts. Not the lifts exactly, but the heights. It sounded like a lot more fun several months ago before snow appeared on Mt. Baldy.

"I don't know, Jim," she hedged.

"Come now. You managed that nasty old lift quite nicely last September when we checked out the aspen. Don't chicken out on me now."

"We'll see."

"We certainly will."

Taylor knew better than to argue with him. He loved a good argument so she changed the subject instead.

"*Casablanca* never loses its appeal, does it? And seeing it in a theatre built before the movie was filmed seems right. I'm so glad they show the occasional classic film."

"You just have the hots for Bogie."

"Really Jim?"

"Where are you parked?"

"In the garage across the street."

"I'll walk you to your car; mine's here on the street."

"Thanks, but that's not necessary."

"Taylor, let no one tell you chivalry is dead. Come along." He tousled her hair like her father used to do when she was a child. She felt about five years old.

"Guess I couldn't stop you anyway," she said.

"That's the spirit."

West San Francisco was crowded with theatergoers. You could tell the Santa Feans from the tourists because they were in a bigger hurry. The locals had to go to work the next day.

They stood for a few minutes waiting for the many pedestrians to clear the front of the theatre. Many streets in Santa Fe were narrow, it was part of the charm, but some barely had room for sidewalks. San Francisco was one way going east and the long line of cars creeping along were hampered by jaywalkers. Those parked in the street were in for a long wait to merge with traffic. The streetlights gave the whole confused mess a movie set quality. Taylor could imagine a director yelling orders to all the extras.

At Sandoval, Taylor and Jim crossed the street and marveled at the massive El Dorado Hotel catty-corner from the garage. It was a mammoth building. Some locals complained it blocked the views and its architecture was not authentic. When they entered the parking structure, Jim waved at the attendant. He seemed to know everyone in town, and could talk extensively about nothing with anyone.

Her blue RAV4, Electric Storm Blue, according to the dealer she bought it from, was parked on the second floor.

"You know, Taylor, a ski rack would look real nice atop the mighty four-by," Jim said as they rounded the turn in the stairs and came out on the second level.

"Good night, Jim." She refused to let him guide her into another conversation about skiing tonight.

"Thank you for seeing me to my car."

"All my pleasure." He cupped her chin. She hated it when he did that. Jim strode off full of himself in his quintessential hiking boots, the only shoes Taylor had ever seen him wear. Jim was really quite attractive. His brown hair and shaggy beard, both flecked with a few silvers, were unruly in the most becoming way. Clear blue eyes twinkled even when he was angry; this happened more frequently than Taylor liked. But his boyish manner made it hard to be provoked with him for long. Jim knew this.

Taylor fumbled in her handbag searching for her keys. It was full of junk she would never need that made locating necessary items trying. She wished she'd gotten them before Jim left. Several lights were out in the garage and it was causing her to be anxious. Funny, they were all out in one corner, almost as if someone had done it purposefully, probably some kids. Where were those keys?

She froze when she heard the noise, her hand jammed to

the bottom of her purse. What was it? She heard it again; a muffled cry. A sound a frightened child might make. Surely no one would abandon a child in this spooky garage. Her fingers grasped the cold keys and pulled them out as quietly as possible. She wanted the door unlocked before she made any move to investigate. With that done, she walked toward the dark corner.

Taylor peered into the dimness and resisted the urge to run for the safety of her car.

"Is someone there?" she called out.

Her heart was racing well past its exercise target rate, and her mouth was suddenly dry. For a moment she sensed, more than saw, a shadow move in the concrete junction. A soft sound, like something heavy sinking to the floor followed. It reminded her of the muted sound feed sacks made when her grandfather lowered one into the back of his pickup on his Kansas farm.

"Hello. Anyone there?"

This time she was answered by an insistent howl from beneath the car where she stood. It wasn't the voice of a child, but that of a cat. Make that a kitten. The tiny ball of orange fur emerged hesitantly from beneath a red Cadillac, checking the temperature first for friendliness.

"So you're the big, bad noise," Taylor said with relief. "What are you doing hiding out in a parking garage?"

Gold eyes searched her soul for murderous intent and seeing none walked resolutely out into the open. Taylor proffered her hand, palm up, and let the creature sniff her.

"Who are you? Do we have a name?" Taylor switched to the royal version. It seemed natural with animals and children. She stroked the dirty, ratty fur and was rewarded with a robust purr.

"Listen to you. You'll have to go some to beat that purr."

By this time Taylor had passed all sorts of cat tests and the kitten was lying happily across her shoulder. Finally, a real soft touch had come along.

"I guess you don't have a home?"

The determined whimper continued, going in for the kill.

All day the kitten had waited in the garage with only a few lookers, but no serious takers. Most people had walked by without so much as a glance. She was the first one to pick him up.

"You're just a baby," Taylor cooed to him, holding the kitten out to look at his size. "Maybe three months old? How could anyone turn you out? You're coming home with me tonight."

Yes, home run!

As Taylor headed for her SUV, she thought she heard another sound from the corner, but dismissed it as nothing. Obviously, it had been the kitten and not some hidden assailant with malice in his heart. She slid into her car; the orange tabby curled tightly in her lap. At last, he felt secure. Taylor touched the locks and pulled the shoulder harness across her chest.

"Hope you don't get carsick." She patted the tiny head and started the car.

She didn't notice the nondescript white van that followed her out of the garage.

*   *   *

A dusting of snow had fallen earlier in the day giving the night a magical quality. Perhaps stardust looked like this; maybe snow was stardust. Palace Avenue wasn't well lighted at night, most of Santa Fe wasn't, but both of her cars knew the way home and she never missed her turnoff. Taylor aimed the RAV up her drive. It made the steep slope seem level. The kitten stirred in her lap sensing they had arrived at their destination. He started at the sudden clamor of the garage door lifting, but relaxed when the soft hand stroked his back.

"Okay, we're home." Taylor squeezed the remote and the door closed. Her body tensed.

"Oh my gosh! How am I going to explain you to Oscar?"

Something was up. The lap he was sitting on was less comfortable. He purred. It had worked before.

6

"He'll have to understand. After all, he wouldn't want you to be homeless, especially on a night like this. I hope you're a tough little cookie because I can assure you that Oscar will not welcome you with open paws."

Taylor placed the kitten over her shoulder again. This time its tiny hind foot landed deftly on her forearm and he snuggled in.

"Getting comfortable?" Taylor asked the now quiet feline. Her only answer was a nuzzle, in her hair.

Once inside the kitchen she confronted a displeased Oscar. It was way past his dinner time and he was prone to revenge such slights. The Abyssinian paced back and forth tangling Taylor's efforts to walk. He had yet to notice the kitten, but all movement stopped at the first plaintive meow from above.

The Aby turned in his tracks and stared at Taylor and her unbelievable betrayal.

"Before you rip me to shreds," Taylor began. "Let me explain."

Oscar had no intention of hearing any explanations. The fur on his back rose in uncharacteristic rage, followed by his tail fluffing to the size of a baseball bat.

The kitten ignored this horrible display of bad manners and cuddled Taylor as if to say, "She's mine. Possession is nine-tenths of the law."

The kitten took a decided interest when the persistent caterwaul turned into a full-fledged howl from the floor.

"Oscar! I shouldn't have expected anymore but really, I did. Shoo! Out of the kitchen."

Taylor gently pushed him along with her foot while he continued to hiss and growl. He swatted her shoe as she guided him out of the door. Even with the barrier, he was still spitting and sputtering in the dining room. Taylor knew she had broken all the rules for a feline introduction and hoped she could smooth things over with Oscar.

"Look, little one, I have to have you tested for, well, for things. So, the two of you really can't meet up close and personal for awhile."

Taylor set the rigid, frightened cat on the floor.

"I'll make you a nice box to tidy up in and give you a soft towel to sleep on. Tomorrow you go to the vet to get checked out."

By the time Taylor had all his necessities arranged the tabby was busy doing his cat things.

"You cats are all alike. You have the same important things to do, like sniffing corners and rubbing refrigerators."

The gold eyes looked back with all-knowing thoughtfulness.

"Well, consider yourself tucked in. I've got to tend to the wild thing."

Oscar was sitting on her bed like a meatloaf, with all his feet neatly pulled under him, tail wrapped tightly around his body, watching the open door with hostility.

"Now Oscar, this is a rescue," Taylor began her pitch. "You wouldn't know about such things because you come from royal blood and were never without a home. But the tiny commoner in the kitchen has not had the advantages you've had. Try to understand."

He proved his great lack of understanding by turning his back on her.

"Okay, be that way. Tomorrow he goes to the vet. Maybe they can find him a good home."

But Taylor was already thinking that Cheddar would be a good name for him. His fur was the color of cheddar cheese. Yes, Cheddar would be a cute name for that ball of colorful striped fur. She hoped the new owners would agree.

"Did you catch the weather Oscar?" She tried small talk. "Are we in for more snow?"

Oscar's ears twitched but he did not reply. Taylor shut off the light and pulled back the curtain.

"Looks like it's clearing off."

She didn't notice the white van parked across the street.

*   *   *

Detective Victor Sanchez hated getting called out at night. It almost always meant something awful had happened.

This time was no exception. A young woman, late twenties, had been found dead by a couple of hysterical tourists in a downtown parking garage. Their vacation had been ruined. He thought the dead woman's night probably hadn't been too good either. This was the unpleasant side of his job. Fortunately, murder wasn't a frequent occurrence in Santa Fe.

The woman lay on the pavement, head resting on a concrete wheel bump. Blood from her slashed throat stained the pink housekeeping uniform she wore. The white, thick-soled shoes were splattered in red.

"No sign of a purse," the officer on duty said. "Watch is gone though Vic."

Victor squatted in the dingy corner of the garage now brilliantly lit with forensic lighting. He lifted her arm with his gloved hand.

"Impression from her watch is still present. Wonder if she's been dead long?"

"ME can probably tell us," the officer replied. "Looks like the motive was robbery."

Victor rubbed his chin. "I'm not so sure."

CHAPTER 2

The veterinarian clinic parking lot was not yet full at this early hour. Taylor had counted on that. The kitten seemed to know he was going to the bad place, and cried pitifully from the time they left the house. Taylor was convinced that cats had a special instinct that told them when the V-E-T loomed on the horizon. She picked up the small cardboard carrier and poked her finger through one of the holes. An orange nose and one gold eye was all she could see.

Inside the Feline Friends Only office, Dr. Evans was talking with the receptionist. She smiled when Taylor entered clumsily toting the carrier.

"Hello Taylor. I didn't know Oscar was visiting today. Is he okay?"

"Oscar isn't exactly okay, but it has nothing to do with his health. I found this kitten last night and he needs to be checked out. Then I'll try to find him a home."

"Let's take a look."

Dr. Evans was a petite blonde with sleekly coiffed hair. Today she had on a white lab coat and bright plum scrubs.

The inside of the clinic was one brightly colored room after another. Teal, purple and canary yellow seemed to dominate with splashes of black and white in strategic places. Taylor liked the cheerful office. She didn't know if the cats appreciated the colors, but she fancied the lighthearted approach.

Dr. Evans pulled the top flaps of the carrier apart and looked at the tabby kitten.

"He's a pretty one, about three months old, I'd say." She rubbed the kitten's head.

"Linda, would you set up a file for this handsome boy? I'll be in the lab."

"Sure Doc." The young woman replied.

Taylor took the card and completed it. She paused momentarily at the name question and then wrote in "Cheddar."

"You want the feline leukemia test done?"

"Yes," Taylor said. "I don't know how long it will take to find him a home, so I don't want to take any chances."

"Just don't name him," Linda said.

"Why?" Taylor asked.

"Once you name them, they're yours. Trust me, I know." She winked.

"Oh. Too late."

"So I see." She placed the card on her desk. The receptionist giggled as she carried Cheddar to the back for his blood draw.

Taylor left feeling a bit as if she'd done something wrong. Not wrong, but something she might regret. In her heart she knew the kitten was already under her skin. She hoped Oscar's claws didn't end up there too.

*   *   *

Ten minutes later she was rushing through the double doors at Piñon Publishing only a few minutes late for work. Candi waved at her from the reception desk. The look on her face was one of tempered bewilderment. This reaction interested Taylor because Candi had a way of handling even the most strange and exasperating situations without becoming frazzled. This must be something out of the ordinary.

"What's up?" Taylor asked.

"One moment." Candi held up an index finger with a

perfectly polished, very long nail, while she answered another call.

"Okay," she said to someone over the phone and punched a button.

"Taylor, hold onto your hat. Dominique Boucher is in your office."

"What?" Taylor said in amazement. "That's not possible."

Indeed it wasn't. Dominique had been Piñon Publishing's bestselling mystery writer until a few months ago. She had died at the hands of a madman, the accountant for the publishing company. Of this Taylor was certain because she herself had found Dominique's body. Dominique was quite dead. However, if anyone could make it back from the far beyond it would be Dominique.

"Okay, what's the punch line?"

"She's waiting in your office."

"Not Dominique."

"Well," Candi conceded, "she gave her name as Crystal Visions, obviously an aka, but she's a dead ringer for our former author."

"Crystal Visions," Taylor mused. "We contracted with her for her New Age mystery."

Taylor pulled her phone from her purse and checked her calendar.

"Oh gosh, I sure do have an appointment with her this morning, but it was supposed to be later. Great, another unpredictable author; is there any other kind?"

"Perhaps she has a crystal ball with her and could answer that question," Candi teased.

"Very funny." Taylor headed for the stairs. The second floor housed the majority of the staff.

"Morning luv," Jim called from his office. Jim recently moved back upstairs after paying some kind of penance in the basement. His office was across the hall from Taylor's and had stood empty for two years after the former CEO had banned him to the underbelly of the office. When Jessica Endicott took over the company she allowed him back into his upstairs office.

"I've got a story to tell you, but it will have to wait. A new author is waiting for me."

"Oh, you mean Dominique?"

"She's not Dominique. What is this, a conspiracy? Her name is Crystal Visions and she's a new mystery author."

"Taylor my dear." There he went again. She hated it when he used that term of endearment. It meant a joke was coming.

"You do need to branch out into the self-help books. You're meeting far too many strange people with the mysteries. It's bound to leave a mark on your personality."

Taylor ignored him.

"I'm sure she's a very nice person. Her book is quite good—different."

"In that case, I'm sure she won't be a disappointment. You can't miss her. She's the pink mummy."

Taylor shook her head and looked upward. She hurried across the hall. Only the back of the woman could be seen seated in her office. But Crystal Visions appeared to be dressed in layers of pink silk wrapped around her slender body.

"Hello, I'm Taylor Browning." She held out her hand.

"Crystal Visions." Her hand was soft but with a strong grip. Taylor barely noticed because she was shocked at the incredible resemblance to Dominique.

"Your mouth is open, Ms. Browning."

"Oh. I am, uh, sorry. I didn't believe our receptionist. She told me you resembled, well, it doesn't matter. But there is a remarkable ... "

Crystal frowned, obviously not enjoying the comparison.

"Sorry," Taylor said regaining her composure. "Sorry, you had to wait. I had you down in my calendar for ten o'clock."

"I was told the office opened at eight-thirty."

"Well, you were told right." Taylor wondered how any two authors could be this much alike. Crystal was a few years younger than Dominique, but she had the same sleek black hair, beautiful exotic face and free-flowing clothing. Unfortunately, she was also exhibiting similar personality characteristics. Dominique had been a difficult person to work with and Taylor feared Crystal was going to be as well.

"So, is Crystal Visions a pseudonym?" Taylor dropped her purse and a manuscript on her desk and sat down.

"It is my legal name."

"I see." Taylor didn't believe her for a minute but didn't think she would get another answer.

"Well then, did you bring the remaining chapters of *Spirit, Mind & Bodies*?"

"It's not finished yet. Here are five more chapters. I've had pressing matters to attend." She pushed a sheaf of paper and a CD across Taylor's desk.

"You could have emailed this. It didn't require an in-person visit."

"I had to fly this way to get home and decided to stop by to see Piñon Publishing."

"We need the remainder of the book this week. It was noted in your contract."

"And you will have it. I'm on my way home now to complete the book."

"But this appointment was to be an editorial conference," Taylor tried again to retain Crystal's attention.

"The book is not finished, and the ending must not be rushed. Art should never be hurried. The conference can be done another time.

"I've got to go now. I have a plane to catch. And that city to the south is the closest airport with a flight to Phoenix."

"You mean Albuquerque?"

"Whatever. Good day." Crystal was gone in a swirl of pink fabric.

Taylor felt that sensation of all the oxygen being gone, just as with Dominique's visits.

"So," Jim said from her doorway. "What do you think?" He was smirking, enjoying Taylor's befuddlement.

"She's a Dominique clone all right; ticked me off just like Dominique did. Gee, golly, whiz. Must we endure another arrogant artiste?"

"You signed her."

"Thanks for reminding me. She hasn't even finished her book. It was due this week."

"Sounds familiar. What is the story?"

"Story?"

"You said you had a story to tell me."

"Oh yes. Come in. Sit."

Taylor came around her desk and took one of the *equipale* barrel chairs. Each office had a pair of these chairs made of leather and Mexican cedar strips. In her office the backs were painted turquoise and a colorful striped seat pad made it more comfortable. It was Jessica's idea, the new CEO, that the office furnishings reflect the region's southwest style.

Jim set his coffee cup on the pine table between them. Taylor found it at an estate sale. It was beat up in the most attractive way. Two tiny green decorative triangles graced each side of the drawer pull; otherwise it was devoid of any fussiness, except the dents and scratches. An ornate hammered tin lamp on the table provided extra light when needed.

Most of the time she preferred talking with people there instead of sitting behind her desk. Everyone seemed more comfortable that way. It was the rare occasion when she needed the power position behind her desk. The only problem had been where to put manuscripts and other publishing paraphernalia. The table had solved that dilemma perfectly.

"I'm all ears," Jim prompted.

"Jim, you won't believe it." She leaned toward Jim already huddled forward over the chair arm.

"I found the most adorable kitten in the parking garage last night. Right after you left."

"Oh, I believe it. I'd also believe that you took it in. You did, didn't you?" He raised an eyebrow daring her to deny it.

"Well, yes, but Jim, he was cold and lost. I had to."

"Of course you did. And how did good old Oscar react?"

"He wasn't pleased, but I know he'll come around, once I make him understand."

"Understand?"

"Jim, you don't know cats."

"I know Oscar. I also know he won't understand."

"Excuse me guys," Candi said. She still had her telephone

headset on and was twirling the unplugged cord with her hand. "This note just came for you Taylor."

"Thanks Candi."

"Secret admirer?" Jim asked. "Perhaps the good Detective Sanchez has missed you?"

"Really Jim. I haven't seen Victor in weeks."

"I'll leave you then. You probably want to be alone." His voice dripped with sarcasm.

Taylor pursed her lips in disgust at Jim's retreating back. She stared at the envelope, addressed with only her first name, and ripped it open. Maybe it was from Victor. He'd been the detective assigned to the death of Dominique Boucher and Piñon Publishing CEO, Preston Endicott. They'd become close during the investigation.

But it was not from Victor. She had no idea who sent it. The single sheet of typing paper rested on the floor where she dropped it. In a heavy handwritten scrawl it read: "I'm watching you."

CHAPTER 3

The following morning Taylor walked into her bathroom to find confetti toilet paper covering the floor.

"Oh no," she said. "Oscar, is this your handiwork?"

She knew it was. Oscar had always demonstrated his annoyance by shredding paper, and sometimes curtains. As she cleaned it up her thoughts turned to the troubling message.

Yesterday's note had frightened Taylor, but she chose to believe it was from a frustrated writer. Over the past year she had received letters from people unhappy because she had declined, *rejected*, their work. Some had called her unflattering names. It hurt, but she got over it. One told her she had ruined his career and damaged his self-confidence forever. All this, because he had received a standard printed rejection. In the beginning she had tried to write personal notes but time was a premium. Eventually she had given up trying to soften the blow and used the printed cards. This was just another struggling writer blowing off some steam.

She wasn't sure that getting published was any more difficult now than at any other time. It had never been easy, although hard economic times and the proliferation of home computers had resulted in thousands of unpublishable manuscripts. Many people thought writing was easy, when, in fact, it takes years of writing to become proficient.

She felt especially sorry when older people called. They

were desperate because their manuscripts could not be published immediately. Time was no longer on their side and they didn't have the years to start over in a new career.

Some wanted to write a biography about a family member or friend. It was not easy to tell them that only biographies about famous people would sell well enough for a publisher to risk the time and cost involved. And sometimes those weren't interesting either.

Writing is work, requiring self-discipline, tenacity, and experience. She understood rejection. Taylor wrote articles for trade publications and had received more passes than acceptances. After experiencing both sides of rejection she'd concluded that dishing it out wasn't any easier than taking it.

It was a beautiful sunny Saturday and Taylor decided to attend a local psychic fair. She thought a little metaphysical education would make working with Crystal Visions' book more interesting. Taylor knew nothing about crystals, channeling, numerology or New Age thinking. Crystal's opening chapters contained not only murder but vast amounts of metaphysical references that Taylor found fascinating.

"Oscar. Cheddar," she called. "Breakfast."

Cheddar had passed all his tests with flying colors and Taylor had used the sink-or-swim school of introduction. There had been no takers at the vet for the baby and Taylor would admit, to herself, she was glad. The tabby was a nearly perfect feline combination of sweetness, typical cat behavior, and the willingness to please. Taylor prayed that Oscar would come to see these virtues for himself.

Oscar materialized out of nowhere. He'd been pretty clingy since Cheddar had become a resident. His territory had been invaded and he was not a happy camper. Poor Cheddar wanted nothing more than a big brother to play with but Oscar wouldn't hear of it. He hissed and swatted at him whenever he got close, but did not attack him. The rest of the time Oscar sulked in the shadows.

Taylor scratched Oscar's head between his ears, his favorite spot, and was reassured to hear his familiar purr.

"Can you ever forgive me, guy? He's only a baby. He doesn't know about things like territory and friendships."

Oscar ate his breakfast, but not with the usual gusto. When the kitten pushed in for a bite from his bowl Oscar smacked him a good one. Cheddar backed off, properly admonished.

"Here, Cheddar. This is yours." Taylor placed a bowl of kitten food on the floor across the kitchen. She stroked his back. Cheddar was delighted. Life was good.

She sighed as she looked at the walls of her breakfast nook. The wallpaper was in various stages of removal. It looked downright tacky with ragged strips dangling bravely from the plaster. She was trying to concentrate on one room at a time now—with the hope of seeing a whole room, any room, finished. The scraping was taking longer than she'd planned. The paper remained firmly fixed in many places causing her will to waver.

"Well, guys, you're on your own. I'm off to explore the New Age. Try not to tear up the house or each other."

Taylor chose her '67 Mustang for the outing. She looked up at the ski basin while waiting for the light to change, and speculated about her fate in Jim's hands high above the city on Mt. Baldy. Jim would insist on taking her skiing. She wanted to go, really, but there was her fear of falling.

A few minutes later she parked the classic red Ford, allowing sufficient distance between two newer, but inferior cars in the Ft. Marcy Park lot. Magers Field was adjacent. Covered bleachers stood behind home plate flanked by terraced banks. Lights soared high above the baseball field. Grass, a rare commodity in Santa Fe, covered the field.

The park provided recreation, exercise classes and a swimming pool in addition to the baseball diamond. For walkers there were landscaped trails with bridges spanning the arroyos. And for canine friends, a dog park with agility course.

Taylor tugged the bulky, burgundy sweater down over her denim clad hips, and threw the shoulder strap of her purse in place. The crisp air invited deep breaths. She'd read in one of Piñon's self-help books about mountain air. It was supposed to encourage positive thoughts and feelings. She couldn't argue with that. At seven thousand feet, Santa Fe had the kind of high mountain air the author had written about.

The psychic fair's white tents were made colorful by Tibetan prayer flags, mandalas and chakra body energy maps. Everywhere there was the aroma of incense. The tents were staked throughout the south side of the park, nestled among the piñon and chamisa. The trees were sans leaves this time of year, yet they still gave a feeling of intimacy to the participants.

Taylor crossed a wooden bridge, following the sounds of people and the succulent aroma of chile *rellenos* on a stick, funnel cakes and cotton candy.

The park was crisscrossed with *arroyos*, dry this time of year. Deciduous trees grew near the banks, waiting their opportunity for a drink. Most would have to wait for the snow cover soon to come.

There were perhaps thirty small tents and many more booths, each displaying signs describing the exhibitors. Taylor paid eight dollars and picked up a program. The back cover page contained a hand-drawn map of the fair. The list of exhibitors was extensive, including artisans selling crystals of purported magical powers, herbalists, aroma therapists, handwriting analysts and palm readers. A massage therapist gave fifteen-minute rub downs. Several workshops on channeling, color readings, automatic writings, and dream interpretation were being held in larger tents.

Taylor chose fliers describing reflexology, spiritual growth and astrology. The New Age was far more complicated than she'd realized. But she wanted to experience something first hand and decided to consult with the palm reader, palmistrist as the program called it.

She stopped at a tent selling herbs. Lying on the counter was a list of herbs, uses, and prices. Under a listing for pets was something called val extract reputed to calm animals. She immediately thought of Oscar but judged nothing would calm him enough to accept the exuberant Cheddar.

Kids were running about in the carnival atmosphere of the fair. One particularly industrious little brat was busily sticking cotton candy in his younger sister's hair. She was shrieking in joy, picking off small tacky pieces of the pink stuff and poking it in her mouth. Taylor was certain her mother would be shrieking later—not with joy.

At the color therapy tent she discovered from the printed materials, left by the absent exhibitor, that the burgundy she was wearing acted to balance the emotions. Her other favorite color, purple, seemed to enhance ESP, encourage spiritual growth and help liberate undesirable habits. She thought wickedly of giving Jim a purple sweater for Christmas. Maybe it would stop some of his undesirable habits.

Sabrina, a spiritual counselor, was doing a booming business. Several people waited in line outside her tent for past life spiritual readings.

Instead of waiting in line, Taylor ducked in the next tent. Here people were allowed to browse. It was her favorite activity—looking at books. These were all metaphysical in nature and covered everything from astrology to Zen.

"Please let me know if I can help you," the attendant said. Taylor thought him well-suited for the New Age. His hair was brown and long. He wore jeans with a tunic style jacket, and faded tie-dyed T-shirt. He tapped on an ancient portable typewriter while conversing with customers. Taylor would have sworn it to be a manuscript. Well, not surprising, everyone was a writer these days.

The choice of books was overwhelming so Taylor left to do some more looking. Maybe she could make a selection later. When she left, he closed the tent.

Taylor moved on to the gem and crystal booth. The display consisted of five-inch square wicker baskets of like stones. Each held a hand-printed calligraphy card describing the properties of each stone. She picked up a piece of malachite. This card cautioned that malachite gives off a toxic vapor when wet. Taylor made a mental note not to wash it. The beautiful egg-shaped stone with the swirling green colors was so intriguing, Taylor bought one.

"Ah, this is a nice one," the woman manning the booth said. "Malachite has the potential to protect us from danger and to enhance one's psychic abilities." Taylor smiled at the thought, not sure what she was getting into. "In fact," the woman continued. "Malachite will shatter to warn of imminent peril."

"Seriously?" the woman nodded. Taylor didn't know whether she was being gaslighted or to take her at her word.

She paid for her crystal and then stopped to look at Apache tears on her way out. She examined first the polished stone, held it up to the sunlight and saw the tear inside. Some unpolished stones were available too, and beautiful in their own way, a rough mixture of black frosted in white.

The tiger's eye was a lovely stone of warm browns, but came in other colors as well. It was good for focusing and self-confidence. Taylor replaced the stone. She was happy with her purchase.

As she walked in the general direction of the palm reader, weaving her way around people, trees, and booths, she failed to notice the man following her.

The palmistrist, Anna, held out her hand to receive the twenty dollars Taylor offered. She placed it in a metal money box on the ground. Taylor watched while the fiftyish woman carefully examined her hand. Anna was plain, wore no makeup, and dressed in an unremarkable pink knit polo shirt and jeans jacket. Taylor was a bit disappointed. She had expected someone more like Crystal Visions, but this woman had no turban, dangling earrings or excessive jewelry on her hands.

The palmist turned her hands gently. The backs of her hands were examined first. "You've been taking medication." Anna's voice was husky—deep. "You should stop it now." Taylor hadn't the slightest idea what she was talking about. The only thing she had taken was vitamin C, for a cold.

"It has become too concentrated. Your ailment is over. You don't need it anymore." Taylor would discontinue the supplement.

The handwriting analyst in the next booth took two bills from a man who seemed more interested in the young woman having her palm read than in having his handwriting analyzed.

"Write this please." He handed the man a clean sheet of

paper, pen and a card with a typewritten sentence to copy. "Copy this, please; and no signature. Signatures are too practiced and rarely reveal the real personality," he explained. Most people wanted to know why.

"Good thing," he said gruffly. While he penned the sample he was preoccupied with Taylor who stood several feet from him. He continued to send searching looks in her direction. He shoved the writing sample at the analyst, crumpling the paper.

The palmist turned Taylor's hands and gently traced the lines on her palms with a pen. The pen tickled her hands. She wondered how long it would take to wash it off.

"Your lifeline is very long, but sadly, it appears you are divorced?" The woman named Anna looked into Taylor's face and saw her wince. "Widowed?"

"Yes," Taylor said.

"I'm sorry, hon, there will be another relationship soon."

Taylor resented the intrusion into her personal life. She wasn't sure what she'd expected. The woman was probably just guessing anyway.

The thin man with the stringy hair studied the handwriting. He glanced up at his customer, as if to make sure of his conclusion, and was stunned to see a face set like stone. This he had not before witnessed. Usually, people enjoyed this, but not this man. For the first time, he felt alarmed. This man could be dangerous. Once again he checked his findings. Club-shaped end strokes, messy ink, made each word burdensome on the last stroke. The heavy pressure had torn the paper in one area. The aggressive *t* bars didn't quite cross completely and indicated possible violent behavior. His capital *I*'s were small enough to suggest strong feelings of inferiority.

"This indicates a branching of career." Anna traced a line on Taylor's palm. "Are you about to change jobs or have you recently?"

"A little over a year ago," Taylor said. This was weird. This woman seemed to be dead-on, or a very good guesser.

"There is threat. I see circles, and red."

"What's that mean?" Taylor said, irritated and slightly unsettled.

"I can't be certain. Be careful."

Having her palm read wasn't as much fun as Taylor had anticipated. In fact, this latest revelation gave her more to think about than she would have liked. She thanked Anna and began the trek back to her car.

The handwriting expert was immensely relieved when his customer abruptly left; to follow the woman. He knew he would have lied rather than face the man and tell him his handwriting showed evidence of a violent personality. His relief for himself was cut short as he realized the possibilities that might befall the woman. He struggled with the scenario. It wasn't any of his business. Yet, he was in a position of knowledge. Wasn't he morally obligated somehow? Hurriedly, he scribbled a short message on the back of one of his cards, pulled the plastic sheet over his booth opening, and raced after the woman with the shoulder-length auburn hair and dark red sweater.

This had to look innocent. He didn't want the man to see him give her the card. His interpretation of this man's potential was enough to warrant caution. He made straight for the concession stand, passed the pursuer, and bumped Taylor.

"Please excuse." He grabbed her hand to steady her, and slipped the card between her fingers. When he reached the concession he couldn't resist looking back. Taylor didn't see him. She was looking at the card. What he saw caused a sudden chill throughout his body. He would swear the man behind her had murder in mind. The man looked him straight in the eye without blinking. Despite his efforts, he had not managed to cover his attempt to warn her. He turned and ordered a beer trying to act as if he wasn't scared half to death. There was nothing more he could do for the woman, only try to protect himself.

Taylor was confounded by the card she held. It read simply, "Jeopardy is everywhere." The man who had bumped her was nowhere to be seen in the milling crowd. Was this some kind of joke? First, the note at work and now this. She felt terribly exposed—as if everyone knew a secret but her. The other side of the business card read, "The message of handwriting." Before she could read the name she was bumped again.

"Sorry," he mumbled. She could only see his back, covered with a navy jacket. He was attempting to regain his balance before he dropped the Coke cup he was carrying.

Enough was enough. All this was giving her a headache. Taylor made her way through the crowd repeatedly excusing herself. She wanted to go home. Halfway to her car she remembered the card. It was no longer in her hand. She refused to go back. There was a lump of fear in her chest. The path to the bridge pitched dangerously near the *arroyo*. For a moment, vertigo set in and she stepped off the path to steady herself, and then took the longer way through the chamisa to the bridge.

***

The police station was practically out of town but Taylor wanted to see Detective Sanchez so she drove through the traffic on Cerrillos Road; also locally known as motel row. It wasn't as heavy as it had been at Thanksgiving. Santa Fe was between the Thanksgiving and Christmas crowds, but soon it would be clogged with Christmas revelers and skiers looking for hotel bargains and finding none.

She was certain Victor would laugh and make her suffer. And then, she could go home confident there was nothing to fear. She supposed it was necessary to sustain the humiliation so she could feel better.

The building that housed the police department and court administration was a pretty ho-hum structure. It didn't even pretend to be adobe. She'd been here twice before. The first time for a similar indignity, and later on when she and Jim were arrested, detained, for a minor infraction at La Fonda. Okay, so it was a brawl. What the heck, that was an indignity too.

Victor Sanchez strode into the waiting area looking for Taylor. She and Victor had met when Piñon Publishing's CEO had been killed a few months ago. He was the detective assigned to the case. They had struck up a friendship of sorts and Taylor had done a little sleuthing herself much to Victor's unhappiness. It had resulted in her near death at the hands of the murderer. She had missed Victor, but didn't feel right contacting him for something other than business.

When Victor got the call from the front desk saying she was waiting to see him, he immediately felt bad he hadn't called her. He thought of her frequently, but there always seemed to be too much work, the reason he was here on a Saturday, leaving no time for a relationship.

She was easily seen, standing out like the proverbial sore thumb. Taylor Browning was unaware she was a beautiful woman, with penetrating green eyes and shoulder rubbing dark auburn hair. She didn't fuss much with makeup, didn't need it. He liked that, being a straightforward type. There, among the uniformed officers and a few rather rough looking individuals, stood one self-conscious woman. She was twisting a strand of hair, something he'd never seen her do.

"Taylor? Hello," he greeted her. "To what do I owe this unexpected visit?"

"Hi, Victor," she said hesitantly. "Can we talk?" She looked about anxiously.

"Sure. This way." He allowed his hand to cradle her back momentarily as he gently guided her away from the commotion, through the large bullpen, to a glassed-in office in the corner.

"This is one of the interview rooms. We'll have some privacy here."

She nodded, clutching her purse, and sat in the proffered chair.

"Do criminals sit in here?"

"Well, yes. Would you like to go somewhere else?"

"No," she lied. She would have preferred any other place but didn't want to make demands. "Just curious."

"How are you? You seem upset."

"I am upset. Well, not really. Something may be happening." She looked around the prefab office space, with the pencil marks on the walls and smudgy fingerprints on the glass, and cringed. "You know, I expected living in Santa Fe to be quite different: restful, quiet, not at all like it has been."

She was rattled all right. Victor remembered the signs, erratic speech patterns, quick changes of subject.

"Why don't you tell me what's troubling you?" He risked touching her shoulder and was relieved to see her relax.

"I seem to be getting threatening notes. Not threatening really, but sort of threatening. Yesterday there was one from an angry writer, today one at the psychic fair."

"Psychic fair?" Another aspect of her personality. She was full of contradictions, at once conservative and yet leaning to the eclectic. A psychic fair was a bit too eclectic for him.

"I know, you probably think it's stupid, but we have this new author—she writes New Age mysteries—and I wanted to know something about it. Metaphysical stuff. The palm reader told me to watch out for circles and red. I mean, what does that mean?"

"Indeed." Victor could think of nothing else to say.

"Then this guy bumps me and sticks his card in my hand. What does `jeopardy is everywhere' have to do with me? No kidding, jeopardy is everywhere; buses, airplanes, stairs, slick floors, bathtubs. You name it. But what's it got to do with me?"

"What about the note from the writer," Victor asked. "What did it say?"

"I'm watching you. Gives me the creeps, but I get one of those every now and then."

"Did it come in the mail?"

"No, oddest thing, some kid delivered it to our receptionist."

"What else was written on the card?"

"I didn't see it all. At the top of the card was printed `The Message of Handwriting.' I didn't get a chance to read the rest before I dropped the card."

"Why did you drop the card?"

"Someone ran into me. Of course, there was a big crowd."

"What did the man look like who gave you the card?"

"Youngish, maybe thirty. His hand was thin, bony."

"Did you see his face?"

"It happened so fast, maybe."

"Hold that thought. I'm going to get someone. Be right back."

In a few minutes Victor returned with a tall, heavy-set man. His mustached face betrayed a kind nature and his eyes fixed upon Taylor in a soothing manner.

"Taylor, this is Detective Anderson. He does the composites you see in the paper. Maybe he can help us get an idea of what this man looks like."

"Please call me Bill," he shook her hand. He carried a laptop that he set on the table. He opened an app.

"Now, what can you remember about the man in question?"

"I didn't see him for long. As I told Victor, Detective Sanchez, he was young and thin."

"Let's start with face shape."

"Slender and long," Taylor said.

He chose a face and added it to the screen.

"What about his hair? Brown, blonde?"

"Blonde. Definitely, and stringy. Thin even."

Bill Anderson clicked on the hair choices and allowed Taylor to evaluate them.

"More like this one."

"Did you notice his eyes? Small, slits, round, large?"

"Round and large. I think his lids were puffy, like someone with a cold."

"Okay." He chose several and let her see each on the face. Taylor looked closely.

"That one." She pointed.

With the eyes in place on the face the composite began to take shape.

"I don't remember anything else," Taylor said. With all the mysteries she read why couldn't she think to note someone's description?

"That's okay, happens all the time," Detective Anderson said. "I'll try several. Frequently, when I get the right one, a person recognizes the suspect. For some involved in a violent crime it can be a traumatic experience." He placed a pair of full lips on the face.

"How's that."

"No, I'm sure he didn't look like that."

"How about thin lips?"

"Yes, but I believe he almost didn't have lips."

"More like this?" He paused for her inspection.

"I think so."

"How about his nose? Big, small, slender?"

"I don't recall. I'm sorry."

"No problem."

Once again he clicked on several for her to choose.

"Let's try the slender one. Since he seemed so thin perhaps his nose was too."

"Is this him?" He turned the computer toward her for a closer look.

"It could be. It really could be."

"Let's get someone out to this psychic fair to look for this fellow," Victor said. Detective Anderson nodded and left the office.

"Wait a minute," Taylor interjected. "I don't know that he's done anything."

"It's just a precaution. If we find him we'll ask a few questions and probably let him go."

"This is not what was supposed to happen," she said.

Victor rubbed his chin as he considered the statement.

"I don't follow."

"You're supposed to smile smugly, offer a few platitudes and send me home. This can't be anything. Right?"

"I'm not sure," Victor said. "Better safe."

"Victor. I don't feel better at all."

"Listen to me." Victor placed his hands on her shoulders. "It's probably nothing, but you know the old saying about where there's smoke? There's a bit of smoke here and I don't want to take any chances. Now, go home, and try not to worry. I'll call you if we turn up anything."

She was about to leave when he spoke once more.

"For once, you did the right thing. You called me."

Taylor smiled at the detective. He referred to her penchant for getting neck deep in trouble before calling in the cavalry.

Taylor walked to her car passing in front of a white van. The driver watched her.

CHAPTER 4

It was a gloomy Monday. Not your typical sunny Santa Fe weather. Snow was due later in the day, six inches perhaps, more in the ski basin. This would prompt more invitations from Jim to accompany him to the slopes. Taylor loved the snow, and she felt she would enjoy skiing when she was better at it. It was the getting better part that seemed to take a millennium.

Strangely enough, for a Monday morning, someone—a guest—was in the office. Piñon Publishing didn't have much through traffic but when it did most people came in the afternoon. Monday mornings were reserved for waking up and a general staff meeting where updates of books in progress were made over strong coffee or tea. But for one notable exception, the senior editor, everyone seemed to be a night owl.

A tall, dark-haired man, in his mid-thirties was chatting amiably with Candi. He was handsome, make that drop-dead gorgeous, and Candi seemed to be taking her time, and batting her very long lashes at every opportunity. He ducked his head bashfully and handed her a sheet of paper.

"I'd appreciate it if you'd give this to the art director," he said.

"My pleasure, Mister?" Candi was piling the helpfulness high.

"Eric. Eric Powers. Thank you ma'am." He had a soft,

pleasant accent. Almost no one Taylor had met was a native Santa Fean, so accents abounded. It was part of the charm.

"Thanks for coming by," Candi cooed.

"Good morning." Eric Powers nodded, including Taylor in the greeting, as he left the darkened office.

Taylor switched on a nearby lamp. "Why is it so dark in here?"

"Because I was a few minutes late and haven't had time to light the works yet," Candi said. "Then the hunk-of-the-month dropped by to grace us with his resume, and well, what can I say?"

"He was pretty, all right."

"Speaking of pretty, have you met the new business manager?"

"Didn't know we had one."

"Virginia hired her while Jessica was out of town. Jim's been showing her around. Anyway back to the pretty part, she fulfills that description perfectly."

"Must be qualified. Virginia's no pushover. But, it doesn't quite sound like Virginia," Taylor remarked. Virginia was a plain woman, with a no-nonsense approach, not given to things fussy or ornamental.

Laughter from Jim's office reached Taylor from the top of the stairs. She stopped at a good vantage point and looked into his office. All she could see was the woman's back. She had long, brunette hair. Jim had a rather sick look on his face, and he was smiling way too much.

"Taylor." His welcome was enthusiastic, far more than necessary. "Come in. Meet Penelope Lane. She's our new business manager."

"Penny, please call me Penny." The lovely, and young, woman took her hand and shook it warmly.

"Penny, how do you do?" Taylor said but her mind couldn't help registering that it was just too cute; a CPA named Penny.

Jim, who was a huge classic rock fan thanks to his father, asked: "Have you heard the song by the Beatles called *Penny Lane*?"

"What? No," Penny replied.

Jim looked perplexed. Obviously, this delectable creature was not quite perfect.

"It was a huge hit during the 'sixties," he explained lamely.

"Oh? Well, that was pre-me." It was a well aimed jab. Jim's gasp was almost audible.

"Penny's filling the vacancy Don ... uh, Mr. Lovitt, left." Jim quickly recovered, and purposefully avoided mentioning the reason for Don's departure. Don was filling his days at the state penitentiary after being convicted of killing Dominique Boucher and Preston Endicott, Jr. Then there was the attempted murder of Taylor herself. She'd never again believe that stuff about mild-mannered accountants.

"She's taking the office next to mine," Jim said.

"The meeting room?"

"It's been moved downstairs to Lovitt's old office."

"When did that happen?"

"Weekend," Jim said. "Must have been a major feat getting the super to come into the building and move furniture."

"I hope you enjoy working here." Taylor remembered her etiquette.

"Taylor, we're going to lunch later. Why don't you join us?" Penny asked. Taylor saw the look of disappointment on Jim's face so she quickly agreed to accompany them.

"Jerk," Taylor muttered in her office. He's making a complete ash of himself she thought. Wasn't that just like a man?

She called Candi on the intercom and asked if there had been any messages from Crystal.

"Not a one," Candi replied. "Jessica had me try her too, but I've only talked with her machine. Want me to try again?"

"No, but thanks."

After several fruitless attempts to reach Crystal she wandered down the hall to talk to Virginia. Virginia Compton was senior editor at Piñon Publishing; although she was fulfilling the duties of editor-in-chief, Jessica refused to give her the title or salary. Jessica still harbored feelings of anger and suspicion when it came to Virginia. She surmised that her dead ex-husband had an affair with the bland editor. Taylor couldn't for the life of her, figure why it mattered to Jessica. There had been no love lost between her and her ex-husband.

The flame-haired CEO's only contributions thus far seemed to be the company change of name, and the ability to keep the staff in a state of fear and dread. This she accomplished through intimidation and thoughtless business decisions. Most of the time she was missing in action; gallivanting about the country. This left pressing matters and day-to-day publishing functions to those remaining. In particular, Virginia, who shouldered huge responsibilities but had no real power.

Taylor was surprised to hear Jessica's voice coming from Virginia's office. Virginia did her best to avoid Jessica, preferring to ignore her presence entirely, but there came a time when she could no longer be pooh-poohed. Apparently, that time had come.

"I don't care if she does have an MBA, she doesn't have any experience." Jessica's voice was rising, the way it usually did whenever she held a conversation, confrontation, with Virginia.

"You didn't give me much to work with, Jessica," Virginia said quietly. "The salary offer was not enough to attract anyone with experience."

"Look, it's an employer's market. There are experienced MBAs begging to be hired at any price. You didn't try hard enough. I can't trust you to do anything right."

"Then perhaps you should do something yourself."

Taylor couldn't believe her ears. Was Virginia leaving the cloak of security and propriety behind and taking a stand?

Jessica was not about to let it go.

"That's sounds like insubordination to me."

"Jessica, you know that you're gone a great deal." Virginia sounded tired.

"How dare you criticize me?"

She knew it was wrong to listen but she felt compelled to do so. Somehow this company had to get back on track or they would all be without jobs.

"I'm only stating the obvious. It's impossible to run a company if you're rarely present to tend to it. We all try to do what we can but authors, vendors and creditors are asking questions that no one but you should be answering."

Virginia was trying. Her tone was at once patient and almost kind, though Taylor knew no benevolence existed between the two. Virginia was interested in the survival of the company. It was everything to her, her entire reason for living.

"What's up?"

Taylor started, embarrassed she'd been caught eavesdropping, and turned to face Alise, Jessica's secretary. She didn't know her very well and wasn't sure if she could trust her with her indiscretion, so she half-lied.

"I wanted to talk with Virginia, but I think she's meeting with someone."

Alise had come to the company at the time of the first murder. She had been all set to leave her obnoxious boss, Preston Endicott, when he was found dead. Although she didn't like Jessica much, at least the boss was gone most of the time and she could Tweet, look out the window, or if she was careful, even do her nails. She had to watch old lady Compton. She was always looking down her nose at her.

"They're going at it again," Alise commented dryly. She sat down at her desk and shuffled paper.

"Guess I'll come back later," Taylor said unnecessarily.

Outside her office she glanced across the hall and saw Jim hanging pictures on Penny's walls. Taylor felt a pang of unwanted jealousy. She and Jim were only friends. Nonetheless, his step was light. What next? Whistling? There was that twinge again.

By lunch, Taylor had done a preliminary edit on the new chapters of *Spirit, Mind & Bodies*. The protagonist was of undetermined age and the owner of a metaphysical bookstore, complete with crystals, incense, herbs, and Tarot cards. The character was becoming involved with the death of a noted businessman. Taylor couldn't wait to read the remainder of the book. Crystal Visions was a talented writer with obvious knowledge of her subject matter.

Originally Taylor was surprised Virginia had agreed to publish the book. But, of course, later she found that she hadn't.

Jessica had given her the assignment, not Virginia. Normally, the sequence of events was that Virginia, being the senior editor, chose the manuscripts to be published. Knowing she hadn't, made the growing dissension understandable. She remembered Jessica had hedged when she asked if Virginia liked the book. Virginia hadn't seen the manuscript. This could mean trouble ahead. From what she overheard that was all any of them needed.

*   *   *

It had begun to snow lightly. Although Del Charro was a restaurant and bar in the Inn of the Governors hotel, it was a popular hangout for locals as well, known for its burgers. The bar was situated on the corner of Alameda and Don Gaspar with windows looking out at both streets. Decorated in lots of leather and wood, it had more of a western look than Santa Fe style. It was a good place for Taylor and Jim because of its proximity to the office. They sat inside the bar, their attention split between the snow falling outside and the massive fireplace. It was cold outside, but Taylor's chill was due to Jim's attentiveness to Penny. She didn't like this aspect of her own personality. The fire gave, at least, the illusion of warmth.

"What's your favorite margarita?" Jim asked Penny. "Taylor's is lily of the valley." He threw Taylor one of his famous sneers. Penny just looked puzzled.

"Jim! For heaven's sake." Lily of the valley had been the poison of choice for Donald Lovitt. She couldn't believe Jim's lack of taste, even though he had demonstrated it many times.

"Private joke?" Penny asked feeling uncomfortable at being left out.

"Not a funny one," Taylor retorted glaring at Jim. "I'll have a house margarita," she told the server. "And a bowl of green chile chowder."

Lunch went downhill after that. Penny refused to try any of the local dining specialties, citing an aversion to anything spicy. She, instead, described her many awards and degrees in detail—she'd gone to Harvard on scholarships, excelled at everything, and graduated with honors upon receiving her MBA. Jim made all the right noises and responded with tales of his many artistic honors and one-man shows. It was all rather nauseating. After inhaling her soup, Taylor excused herself and left Jim to cope alone.

The Plaza was peaceful as her boots made crunching sounds in the snow. It was coming down harder now and the square was nearly empty except for the vendors at the Palace of the Governors. They were almost always there. She walked under the vast *portal* of the Palace past Native American craftsmen wrapped in hand-woven blankets, with jewelry, pottery, and sand paintings spread before them. They weren't busy today. Only two hardy tourists struggled to make selections. Taylor said hello to the artisans she recognized.

Taylor did not rush. She loved winter. Santa Fe averaged about thirty inches of snow per season, much more in the mountains. Snowflakes floated gently to her face where they melted leaving moist droplets. It lightened her mood and far too soon she finished the short walk to the office.

She collapsed in her chair, closed her eyes, and rubbed her aching head. Was it the margarita or the luncheon chitchat that caused her head to hurt? After a few minutes she noticed the envelope. A plain business-sized #10 addressed to "Taylor Browning." She pushed her chair back with a forcefulness that surprised her.

"Not another one!" With great trepidation she opened it. A plain piece of copy paper had a single sentence written on it. "I'm closer than you know."

CHAPTER 5

With shaking hands, Taylor tried to dial Victor's number at the police station. Her index finger kept hitting the wrong numbers. After two tries she dropped the receiver on her desk pad. The unmistakable sound of Jim's clomping boots sounded on the staircase.

"Jim," she yelled. "Please come here!"

"What is it?" The alarm in her voice brought him in a hurry. "Are you okay?"

She handed him the crumbled paper.

"It's the second one I've received."

He read it quickly.

"My god! When did you get the first one?"

"The day you were in my office. Remember? You teased me about a secret admirer."

"Taylor," he exclaimed, "why didn't you tell me you were really concerned?"

"Because I was afraid you'd tease me."

"Have you told Victor?"

"I told Victor about the other one ... and the psychic fair. Next thing I knew I was sitting in a grubby office at the police station playing with eyes and noses, putting together a composite of this guy."

"What guy, and what psychic fair?" his eyebrows rose in amazement. "Really, Taylor, what have you been up to?"

"It was after I had my palm read."

"Your palm read?" A grin broke across Jim's face. "Sanchez must have been humoring you. No one believes that stuff."

"Thank you very much." Taylor was hurt. Jim wasn't going to take this seriously.

"Look, this guy bumped me on purpose and stuck his card in my hand. He'd written a warning on the back, something about jeopardy. A few minutes before, the palm reader told me to watch for the color red and circles. She said I could be in peril."

"Red and circles? Red and circles! Give me a break, Taylor." He spread his arms and formed a circle. "That stuff's all a sham."

"Look, Jim, if you're going to make light of this, then just go away." Tears filled her eyes and threatened to pour forth at any second. She tried to swallow the lump in her throat.

"Here," he pulled a tissue from the box sitting on her desk. "I'm sorry; didn't mean to make you feel worse. This kind of thing happens from time to time. Virginia's gotten a few letters from ticked off writers. It goes with the territory; can't make all the people happy all the time. You know that."

"Do you really think so?" Taylor felt like the wimp of the year. Jim was right. It was a disappointed writer. When he, or she, tired of the game it would stop.

"Taylor, are you there?" Candi's voice burst over the intercom. "Line two for you, Detective Sanchez."

Taylor wiped carefully at her eyes, and smiled weakly at Jim.

"Should I tell him?"

"Do you want to spend another two hours looking at noses?" He left.

"Hello, Victor."

"Good news. We've brought in the handwriting analyst; one Josef Ray. Got a string of priors; minor violations. Can you come down and identify him?"

She didn't want to. "Okay," she answered reluctantly, "I'll leave right away."

"See you soon."

"Victor ... when was he picked up?"

"Right after lunch. Why?"

"No reason. I'll be there in thirty minutes." Taylor felt huge relief. The guy could have left the envelope while she was at lunch with Jim and Penny. That had to be it. There wouldn't be any more. Victor had the man in custody.

***

"He wants to talk with you," Victor said as he ushered Taylor through the crowded receiving area. "You don't have to, but he insists you're in danger. Not from him, of course. It's probably an effort to divert blame to someone else."

"I'll see him."

"Are you sure?"

"Yes, I want this to be over."

"Okay, this way." He led her down a long narrow hall. The brown tile looked dingy in the harsh fluorescent lights. Dirt and sweat clung to the once white walls where humanity had left its mark in close quarters.

Josef Ray sat in a small office used for interrogation. It was similar to the one she'd sat in earlier while making composite faces. However, this room had no windows. A single grey metal table with a white Formica top stood squarely in the middle of the room. Four padded chairs, sans arms, were arranged two and two across the table. Taylor immediately felt the claustrophobia suspects must feel upon entering a room the size of a closet. She felt compelled to confess to anything just to get out of there. Instead she suppressed her consternation and took the chair facing Josef Ray.

His wispy dark blonde hair hung limply over faded blue eyes; eyes accustomed to trouble. His bony, pale hands wrung in silent agony while he waited for fate to take its course. Taylor had remembered his description better than she thought possible.

Ray thought Taylor a pretty woman, average in height and weight but definitely not average in looks. Not many women had auburn hair, a standout in a sea of blondes and brunettes. However, there was a certain something about her that engaged him. She had classiness about her, carefully, intentionally, hidden in simple clothes and casual manner. He hoped she did not fear him. Somehow he had to make her understand he was not a threat.

"This is the card you were given at the fair?" Victor handed her a beige business card. "The message of handwriting" was printed in black script at the top, "Handwriting Analysis by Josef Ray" in bold letters across the center. There was a website URL in the lower right corner.

"Looks like it." She placed it in her lap.

"This is Josef Ray. Is he the man who gave you the card at the fair?"

"He could be." She felt uncomfortable staring at him. The man didn't seem to possess an ounce of malice. He had a refugee look, sunken eyes and emaciated body. She hoped the man was not ill. He certainly looked sick—and frightened. Taylor couldn't help feeling sorry for him. How hard things must have been for him.

"May I say something?" he asked.

Victor got up abruptly and asked the officer outside the door to join them. "You don't have an attorney present," he told Ray. "Are you sure you want to talk without one?"

"Yes."

"Very well."

"You may be in danger," he told Taylor. "While you were having your palm read there was a man at my booth. He was ... well, I can't be sure, but his writing seemed ... volatile."

"This is ludicrous," Victor scoffed. "Come on." He took Taylor's arm.

"No. Wait." Josef Ray implored. "It wasn't just his handwriting. The man watched her all the time. He looked at her ... I don't know, coldly. Like ice." He shrugged trying to find the most persuasive words. "The pressure of his handwriting was extreme. It exhibited heavy cups."

"Enough," Victor said.

"Please, listen to me," the man pleaded. "You've been receiving notes? Let me look at them. I still have the sample he gave me. I could compare."

"Get him out of here," Victor told the officer.

"Please be careful," he tried once more. "People with explosive personalities often have this type of writing. Let me have a piece of paper. I'll show you what to look for." Even as the officer dragged the poor man away, he tried once more for Taylor's attention. "He was tall, dark hair, artistic hands." He was still pleading with her to be careful as he was taken away.

"Victor, I'm scared. What if he's right?"

"He's just trying to divert attention elsewhere. This guy's wanted for burglary, car theft, and shoplifting. It's probably a ploy."

"What if it isn't?"

"I know this has been a scare, but it's over," Victor said. "We got him."

"But why? If he's the one, why did he want to warn me? What about the note at the office, how did he know where I worked?"

"He's a writer. Did you know that?"

Taylor shook her head, but it didn't surprise her, everyone seemed to be.

"Found manuscripts at his house," Victor said. "Not much of a house—four-room dump—but he had a table set up with an old IBM typewriter."

"Why did he become a handwriting analyst?"

"Maybe the writing wasn't paying off. Who knows, people survive any way they can."

"I got another note," Taylor said casually.

"Today?"

"Yes, after lunch. It was on my desk when I returned."

"That's why you asked when we picked him up?" Victor asked.

"I brought it. Perhaps you could compare his writing with this."

"We'll do that. Of course, he may try to disguise his writing, but our handwriting analyst can attest to its authenticity. He's not psychic, but he's pretty good anyway." His eyes had that twinkle that told her she'd been had.

"Thank you so much," her cool voice replied.

"Sorry. It was a cheap shot. Go home, have some tea, and don't worry."

"It seems that's all you ever tell me. Victor, I am not a child, nor am I a weak, stupid woman. I don't appreciate being dismissed." She stomped, as best she could, from the office. Had she looked, the smile on Victor's face would only have further infuriated her.

*　　*　　*

Victor's smile faded quickly as he watched her walk through the door. His hunch was that Josef Ray was not the problem. There was always the chance he was wrong. He hoped so. He also hoped he could solve the issue quickly, before another note appeared.

CHAPTER 6

"Taaay-lor," Jim sang her name off key over the intercom. Taylor glared at her speaker as if it offended her. "I think I was a little rough on you the other day. You know, about the palm reader and all. Anyway, I want to make it up to you. How about it?"

"How about what?" He was right on. Taylor was miffed at him and Victor, and all the other people who sniff at something just because it's different.

"The ski basin is open. How about I take you for a test drive on the bunny slope?"

"Oh, Jim. I don't know. I'm reading a manuscript today and I'd like to finish it. Besides, it's a work day." The thought of swooshing down a gradually sloping mountainside in the crisp air and sunshine was appealing, if only she could remain upright. She didn't want to give in too easily to Jim. A little encouragement went a long way with him.

"Best time to go. The sun is out, the powder's virgin; the crowds won't be there until tomorrow. Live while the living's good."

"Are you buying lunch?"Taylor asked sweetly.

"I'll spring for lunch. Give in?"

"Okay. Give me thirty minutes to find my ski outfit. Do you know a good, as in cheap, place to rent skis?"

"Do I know a place?" Jim never said goodbye.

Taylor put the manuscript away and drove home. She pulled her several cumbersome ski outfits from the top of her closet: black stretch pants, purple down-filled jacket with teal collar, black leather gloves, and black headband. A teal turtleneck sweater rounded out the ensemble.

She winced slightly as she pulled on the tight fitting pants. "What do you think, Oscar?" The Aby looked up from licking his foot and scrutinized her. "Should I switch to the bib? Everyone looks like a blimp in a bib."

Cheddar entered the room with a shrill "Yeow." Oscar turned his back to him.

"Cheddar, you're younger, perhaps your fashion judgment would be better anyway."

"Good grief, here I am talking to cats again. What do either of you know about cutting a fine figure on a ski slope?" The question fell on cat ears—the same as deaf ones. Taylor gave one more appraising look in the mirror and decided she looked great; at least good. Better than a lot of folks would look. The doorbell rang making further deliberations moot.

"That's Jim. You guys behave. I'll see you later."

True to his word Jim took Taylor to a ski rental place that fit her budget. "You know, if you're going to live here you should buy your own skis and boots. If you rent very many times you might as well own them."

"Let's see how it goes first. Remember, I am a fledgling, not a true ski bum like you." Taylor chose a pair in her size from the many racks that lined the walls of the shop—white boots for women, grey boots for men. She hoisted them from the shelf onto the indoor-outdoor carpet on the floor and sat on a long bench to try them on. The back of the boot pulled apart and she pushed her right foot down. Once it was closed, her foot felt packed like a sardine. Ski boots are heavy and cumbersome—the soles don't bend—so walking became more exhausting than skiing. The buckles resisted her efforts to close them, as usual.

"Here," Jim said. "Once it's comfortable, just whack the buckle." He demonstrated. The boot relinquished control.

"Great," Taylor said. "Now I'm ready to do the monster walk once we get to the basin."

Taylor had watched in awe as other skiers negotiated the metal steps and obligatory railroad ties at ski resorts. She envied their carefree walk that she had yet to master. Pitching head first was a very good possibility in the clumsy footwear.

"Now for the skis," Jim said.

"How about a pair of 145s," Jim called to the technician. "We've got a beginner here." Shorter skis made turning easier for the inexperienced.

"Coming right up."

Taylor wished he wouldn't announce to the world her tenderfoot status; she despised being inept at anything. Her first attempts at skiing had been humiliating, not to mention bruising. She wondered again why anyone in their right mind would strap boards to their feet and plummet down a mountainside. In Kansas City, when an ice storm came through, walking had been a joke. Some people, including Taylor, had removed their shoes to get traction with their socks, just to get around. The first time on skis had been like trying to walk on ice. What a stupid thing to do. But there were those runs where everything worked right and she was elated to glide freely down a hill without mishap. Those moments made it all worthwhile.

While Jim watched the technician adjust the bindings for her height and weight, she chose a pair of blue poles, remembering to check for the right angle her arm made as she held the poles in her hands. They were too tall and she reached for a shorter pair. Just right.

"Guess they're getting a jump on the crowd too," Jim mentioned as a white van followed them out of the tiny parking lot.

As Artist Road gave way to Hyde Park Road and the elevation increased, piles of plowed snow rested in smooth heaps at the pavement's edge. The road itself was wet but clear, thanks to the bright sunshine. Piñon and chamisa gave way to towering ponderosa pine, Douglas fir and the aspen forest.

With each 1,000 feet they ascended the temperature dropped three to four degrees.

Taylor pulled down the visor mirror and smeared sunscreen across her nose and cheeks. Her skin was fair and without blemish. She wanted to keep it that way.

"Never use that stuff," Jim said from behind the wheel. "Prefer the raccoon look."

"What?"

"White circles around the eyes where my sunglasses sit. The rest of my face tans."

"That must be attractive. Will I be witness to this sight by the end of the day?" Finally, something to tease Jim about, and he'd set himself up perfectly.

"We'll have to wait and see," he said warily.

The parking lot was crowded but not like it would be later after all the runs opened. It was the first week in December. Thanksgiving had been a disappointment to skiers. Not enough snow. But several storms in the mountains over the past week had allowed a limited number of runs to be opened.

They trudged over the pavement and up the steps to buy lift tickets. After standing in that line, they moved to another line, slammed boots to skis, and waited on the Super Chief quad lift. They slid their skis a couple feet at a time as each chair swept four people away. When their turn came, Jim said, "Take a deep breath, and don't look down."

"Where do you propose I look while being carried to certain death on a ski lift?"

"Enjoy the view."

They sat back in the lift with another couple and it swung smoothly out of the loading zone.

"Nice thing about these quads; they're so steady. Barely bump, even at the towers."

Little reassurance for Taylor who was gripping the safety bar for all she was worth. Jim caused her further apprehension by gently swinging his legs. She glared at him and he stopped.

Near the top she rehearsed in her head what Jim had taught her about getting off the lift. Learning to do this smoothly had been a hard-won victory after she had fallen time and again. The beginner's tendency was to stand upright, but that technique had landed her on her backside every time. Finally she had disciplined herself to squat slightly and immediately shift her weight to turn away from the lift area. Frequently a pileup of colorfully clad bodies would occur at the top of the beginner hill.

The icy bump at the end of the lift loomed ahead. Jim lifted the safety bar and Taylor felt as if her lifeline had been removed. She carefully slid forward in the seat as the chair approached the top, holding her poles in her left hand, her right still attached to the chair. With a small thud her skis met the slick packed snow and she rose slightly, leaving her knees bent. It had been at least a year since her last skiing attempt and she felt wobbly. At the last possible moment she released her grip on the chair and allowed herself to slide down the incline and ski out of the way.

"Excellent dismount," Jim whooped. "At the top and still standing."

"Not too bad, if I do say so myself." Then she admonished herself for getting cocky. She'd pay for that.

They made a right, moving out of the way as other skiers came off the lifts in fours.

"This slope meanders around and back to Lower Broadway," Jim said. "It's beginner all the way."

Taylor pushed with her poles and followed Jim who quickly outdistanced her. This area was a bit steep for her and she carefully eased into a snowplow stance and made long, diagonal sweeps, crisscrossing the wide slope. She concentrated on each turn. Weighting her right foot caused her to turn left. Somehow it seemed backwards to her so she took her time.

The snow had been groomed but with so few skiers it had yet to become packed. It was perfect snow, good traction for a beginner and yet fast enough for some thrills. The white stuff crunched beneath her feet and she delighted in the one thing Dave had never been a part of. It was sad he had died before they could learn together. He would have loved it. But because it was hers alone, it had acted as an independence builder for

Taylor. Nothing had given her the feeling of exhilaration like skiing—not since she had ridden fast horses as a girl.

"You're doing great!" Jim yelled up at her. "What's this I hear about you not being able to ski? Looks to me like you do just fine."

"Thanks. For a novice you mean?"

"A good novice. You may be ready for intermediate runs sooner than you think."

"No hurry." Taylor narrowly made the last turn before she reached Jim. She slid awkwardly to a stop next to him.

"Why don't you go on and catch me next time you come down."

"Hey, I don't mind hanging out."

"Jim, you're an advanced skier stuck on a bunny slope. You go on. I'll do better without an audience anyway."

"Okay. See you in a few minutes. Be careful." He flashed her a smile and was off.

The trail narrowed to the size of a country road as Taylor made the turn onto the run called Thru Way. She supposed the runs could be used as access roads during the summer to maintain the basin; she knew the snowcats used them to groom the slopes, leaving their "cat" tracks in the snow. Taylor continued to make her way back and forth across the run, skiing slightly up the banking to slow her speed and maintain control. When the run flattened she practiced parallel skiing to gain some speed. Her hair flew back from her face and the wind felt frosty. She was enjoying herself.

When the trail forked, she took a right. She finished the run Lower Broadway and found herself back at the lift area. Jim was nowhere to be found, so she caught the lift with three giggling college girls and made two more trips to the base by herself. She fell once on the third run, picked herself up and continued.

The sun glistened off the snow. The pines groaned under the load of white, looking like fluffy giants. Taylor enjoyed the sharp air and warm sun. She paused momentarily to unzip her jacket. Skiing was very aerobic and she was getting a bit tired. At the end of the run, she struck the binding with her pole and released each of her boots. She deposited both skis and poles in the rack that always reminded her of a bicycle rack, and negotiated the steps to the top of the deck to wait for Jim.

At the grill, hamburgers and hot dogs sizzled and popped. The aroma made her ravenous. She pulled some cash from her zippered pocket and bought a hot dog with everything and a Dr. Pepper to wash it down. Hot dogs were her favorite guilty pleasure food, and for a moment she pondered the effects of eating nitrates. She pushed the first bite in hoping for no ill effects. How could anything this mouth-watering cause pain?

"Thought I was going to buy lunch?" Jim's shadow loomed over her and the picnic table she had strategically chosen so she could watch for him.

"Hungry," she muttered around the food in her mouth.

"I guess." He made a beeline for the grill and returned shortly with two hot dogs, extra mustard.

"How'd it go?" Jim took a huge bite.

"Great. Only fell once."

"How many trips?" Between bites.

"Three."

"Good. Good for you."

"You?"

"Took a few blacks but mostly blues. Like to take it slowly at first. In a couple of weeks I'll do the advanced only."

"Show off."

Jim grinned at her. "Jealous?"

"Yes and no."

"How so?"

"Yes, I'd like to ski better, and no, I don't want to do anything along the extreme line."

"Heard from Lady Crystal yet?" He made a right turn in the conversation.

"Nary a word."

"Bet you don't."

"Why not?" Taylor asked.

"Writers."

"Is that self-explanatory?"

"You know yourself how strange they can be."

She grudgingly admitted, "Some writers have a tendency to be their own worst enemies. I can't tell you how many times I've called to tell an author the long-awaited interview has been scheduled only to have her reply that it's the same time as her hair appointment, or that he couldn't possibly do a phoner from a hotel room. Must be fear of success."

"Probably fear of being dim-witted."

"Jim!"

"Ready to tackle the hill again?"

"If I said no, would I be a dim-witted?"

"That's affirmative."

"Let no one say Taylor Browning has any fear of success."

"That's the spirit." He pounded her on the back but she barely felt it through all the down in her jacket.

She wouldn't admit it to Jim, but she knew about fear of success. It was so much easier to fail completely or be safe in mediocrity. Friends and family didn't always cheer on success—too threatening. People who knew you often preferred no changes even if they were for the better. Taylor reminded herself this was a new beginning here in Santa Fe. She didn't need to fear change.

They rode the quad to the top once more. For a moment Taylor caught herself swinging one foot and stopped it quickly before Jim noticed. Too late. He winked at her as if to say she was coming right along.

She staggered a little getting off and Jim steadied her elbow as she recovered less than gracefully but remained upright.

"Thanks," she said.

"You would have made it without me," he said graciously. Every now and then Jim quit being a jerk and turned into a terrific guy. But most of the time his defenses held firm. Taylor had learned to like him anyway.

"Let's take the Santa Fe Trail. The slope travels in a fairly straight line but you can return by several different routes. It's definitely beginner. Just be careful not to make a wrong turn. It intersects both blue and black runs."

"You go. I'll be fine," Taylor said and waved Jim on.

"Okay. I'm going to take a diamond down."

Taylor nodded and pushed off in a series of wide long turns. The trail crossed at least a half-dozen others but she was careful not to deviate from the easy one, pausing to let skiers taking the steeper runs cross her path.

She came to an intersection and slowed to merge with the others. Taylor stopped completely near the opening of a black run called Bozo. Glancing downward she could see nothing funny about it and cringed at the irony. For a few moments she watched the lifts spanning the mountain carrying skiers above her to the top. A small boy shouted to her and waved. It made Taylor smile with envy. Most of the trails on this side of the mountain were advanced. Kids were fearless.

By the time she heard the skier behind her it was too late to get out of the way, even though she tried. It must be some hot dogger without the courtesy to call out. One of the rules of skiing was letting skiers downhill from you know what to expect. Shouts of "On the right!" were common place. The impact was sudden and powerful. Her legs crumpled, her breath was knocked violently from her. Taylor hit the ground hard and found herself sliding on her back along the advanced trail. If she couldn't get control she would crash into the trees and rocks that lined the narrow dangerous slope.

Desperately she flailed her poles, losing one, in an attempt to stop the terrifying speed. Her legs would not, or could not, take orders from her brain. The useless skis were only hampering her efforts to save herself by acting as rudders to nowhere. Her gloved hands could not gain purchase and produced little or no drag. The noise was deafening. The grating sounds the metal edges made on the ice and snow were horrible as she tried to find something, anything, to hold on to. Each time a rock or tree presented itself she would try to push herself away from it with her pole. In the end nothing she could do would stop this. Her strength was all but gone. She could not fight the harrowing descent much longer. Maybe she should just let it happen and stop this crunching and spinning.

Jim was skiing above her when he witnessed the incident.

Taylor was standing near the edge of her run when a skier dressed in a red jacket pushed her out of the way.

"Hey, buddy," he yelled even though there was no way the words could reach the skier. The man was well on his way to a fast getaway but Jim could not bother with that. Taylor careened dangerously near the woods along the run. He watched helpless as he skied with the fall line to what appeared to him to be a hopeless rescue attempt. She was flat on her back, skis askew, and spinning out of control. It would be hard for anyone to get there in time, and little chance of stopping her without adding to the carnage.

Taylor continued to gain speed as she approached the mogul field. The big bumps produced by repeated skiing without grooming were great fun for the experienced skier, but they knocked more air from Taylor's lungs as she plowed through them, becoming airborne between moguls. She tried to wrap her arms around the mounds but they were too icy. Any attempt on her part to wedge her skies into the hollows would probably result in a broken leg.

Jim cursed in frustration as he left the trail and went kamikaze through the trees taking a short-cut to Taylor. The snow was deep here and slowed him enough to make the essential turns to avoid hitting the snow-laden pines. He flew up an embankment and took to the air, landing on the groomed slope where Taylor fought to gain control in a never-ending spin downward.

Throughout her life, it seemed to Taylor that just as she was about to give up, something would appear to give her hope. Today it was two bales of straw. She saw them at the moment she was flying headfirst down the slope. Someone had placed them for skier protection where the forest protruded into the run. If she could stab one with her remaining pole she might just stop skidding. The binding on her right ski broke loose and she heard it crack up on something above her. It was probably for the best. She could control her foot better without it. With her last bit of energy she dug in with the heel of her boot and crunched through snow to ice, slowing her in a series of bone-jarring half-halts. It was enough for her to lurch toward the first straw bale. Her pole missed it by inches.

Jim was putting lifelong skills to use as he lunged down the steep, hazardous trail. He glanced quickly at Taylor's sliding body and saw her failed attempt to stab a bale of straw with her pole.

"Hold on!" he yelled unnecessarily.

Neither could she hear or hold on. He negotiated the moguls in his path by making quick turns, but no way was he going to be fast enough to get to her in time. If she missed the next bale she was going to be hurt—if she wasn't already.

Taylor had to pierce the next bale or she'd be a pile of broken bones. She tried to brush away the snow covering her face for a better look. Feet first she shoved the metal edge of her one ski as deep as she could, and was relieved to feel the free fall slow. With a groan, because it hurt her arm, she plunged the pole into the bale and hung on for her life. It bowed precariously, bending like bamboo in a stiff wind, as her weight pulled at it. It held. When all motion stopped, except the stars in her head, she was face down with only the strap from her pole holding her in place. Her wrist would hurt for some time from the beating it had taken but she thought nothing broken.

"Taylor!" She had been unaware Jim had seen the whole thing from above. He skidded to a stop in a shower of snow, stepped out of his skis, and plunged them in the snow making an X; the distress signal on ski slopes.

He dialed the ski patrol on his cell but had no signal.

"Get the ski patrol!" he yelled to a passing skier.

"My god, are you all right? That was an awful spill." He carefully felt her arms and legs and turned her face up.

She hesitantly tried all her body parts and everything seemed to work.

"Taylor, lie still. The ski patrol will be here shortly."

"I think I'm fine."

"Does your head hurt? Are you dizzy? Where are they?" He looked upward hoping to see help coming.

"Jim." Taylor sat up and was relieved her head did not hurt. She pulled off her glove and rubbed the wrist that gave of itself so the rest of her might go on living. It was extremely painful and she guessed it would get worse.

"What happened?"

"Some guy in a red jacket, at least I guess it was a guy, slammed into you. Did he call out?"

"Not a word. By the time I realized someone was near, it was too late to get out of his way. Is he all right?"

"All right? Yeah, he's fine. Watched the idiot finish the run and disappear. From my angle it looked like you were deliberately pushed."

Taylor's face looked anxious, her eyes were huge and she was flushed. "He was wearing red?"

"Yes, red ski jacket with a large white "O" on the back. I'll report him for all the good it will do. He's probably halfway back to Santa Fe by now."

"You mean a circle?"

"What?"

"Remember, the palm reader told me to watch out for red and circles?"

"Oh, Taylor, for heaven's sake, this guy ran you down and you're thinking about something some kook said."

She wanted to reply but the ski patrol arrived, packed her in blankets on a small toboggan, and took her down to first aid.

*   *   *

"Don't you see," Taylor explained as she unlocked her front door, "the palm reader's warning has been fulfilled. She was talking about this skiing incident. Now I won't have to worry about it anymore." She was struggling with the key, trying to remove it from the door lock when Jim inhaled audibly.

"Geez, Taylor, you didn't leave this mess did you?"

Drawers were open in the alcove off the foyer. She'd only recently had the L portion of the living room walled to provide for her home office. The wooden doors had been closed over the arched opening when she left. She always closed them to keep her cats from pillaging while she was gone.

"Oh no!" Taylor stifled a scream. "My cats. Oscar, Cheddar," she called.

"Wait, they might still be here."

"Of course, they're still here. They have to be."

Jim gripped her shoulders. "The people who did this may still be here," he said quietly. "We've got to call the police."

"But, my cats. Oscar!"

The door to the deck closed with a thud. Jim pushed through to the living room.

"Jim, don't."

Taylor followed the fool.

CHAPTER 7

Taylor stood among her violated belongings. It wasn't just her new home office that had been trashed. Every room she could see from the living room, where she cowered close to the side door, was a mess. Several drawers in the kitchen were open but the contents had not been spilled. There was no absolute damage, nothing smashed, but complete dishevelment. Everything had been looked at and replaced haphazardly. Her heart ached with the fear that something had happened to Oscar and Cheddar.

Although it had only been a few minutes, it seemed an eternity since Jim disappeared into the chamisa in the backyard. Taylor could not wait another moment to find the cats. She crept toward the closed bedroom door, a door she had left open. Her knees were unsteady and the blood throbbed through her ears. Dare she open the door? Instead of calling the police, her fingers touched the door knob lightly as if testing for heat. A ringing sound, more of a tinkling really, sent sound waves through the door. There was no mistaking—it was coming from the bedroom. The wall provided some safe haven as she flattened herself against it and listened. Taylor couldn't bring herself to open it. She searched her purse for her cell phone.

Oscar's meow stopped the hunt for the phone. He scratched at the door begging to be let out. Slowly, very slowly, she opened it. Oscar squeezed through the small opening, bending his lean body like a snake, and dashed into the hall, rubbing Taylor's legs with an enthusiasm not formerly displayed in his eight years. Taylor scooped his body into her arms and held him close. His huge amber eyes looked out from under the expressive clown markings of his Abyssinian heritage.

"Are you okay, baby cat? What did he do to you?" Around Oscar's neck was a length of string. Two tiny red bells, the kind found on Christmas presents, rang off key every time he moved. She struggled with the string and gave up. It would have to be cut.

"Where's your buddy, Oscar?" The movement at her feet was the tabby kitten, slinking out of the bedroom. Cheddar sniffed the air, decided all was friendly, and stood on back legs, reaching up to Taylor, pawing at her leg.

"There you are!" Oscar didn't care to have the runt this close, but he was plenty distressed so he tolerated Taylor holding them both, one against each side of her neck. Their bodies shook with relief and anxious purring.

"Can't find anyone. He must have hidden in the chamisa." Jim returned through the open glass door, dusting his hands and picking the blue-green foliage from his jacket. "Everyone okay?"

"Seems to be, but this awful thing needs to be cut off." Taylor pulled at the string around Oscar's neck. "Who could have done this, Jim?"

"Anybody. No one has any respect for the property of others. Why work for minimum wage when you can steal smart TVs?" Jim pulled a pocket knife from his pants pocket and quickly sliced the twine collar from Oscar's neck.

"Is anything missing?"

In her happiness to find both her cats safe, it hadn't occurred to Taylor to check. "Well, my dumb TV and DVD player are still here. The laptop is still on my desk. My stereo system consists of an all-in-one player with a couple of small speakers. That's about the limit of my fenceable items. But, Jim, someone went through all my things, and apparently put them back. Sloppily."

"Have you checked the bedroom?"

"No, but the cats were in there."

Jim pushed back the door. The drawers were agape. Her sweaters, lingerie, and nightshirts draped over the sides. The clothes hanging in the closet looked like the leavings of a sidewalk sale. Most of her clothes hung crookedly on hangers, but several items lay on the floor. Jim picked up the phone at her bedside and dialed the police. He gave a staccato report and hung up.

"They'll be here in a few minutes."

"Oh my god." Taylor followed his line of vision to her mirror hanging askew on the wall over the dresser.

In lipstick, very straight to video, was scrawled, "I feel so much closer now."

The phone rang and they both jumped. Jim grabbed it before it could ring again.

"Yes," he barked.

"Who's this?" It was Victor Sanchez.

"Jim Wells."

"Are you always there? Let me speak to Taylor."

"Listen, we just called the police. Something's happened."

"I'll be right over."

"Sanchez," Jim said to Taylor as he replaced the receiver. "On his way."

Victor beat the patrol car by seconds. After surveying the chaos he asked, "Anything missing?"

"I don't think so. I'll know better after I clean up the mess," Taylor replied, looking once again at the state of her home.

"Sanchez, what about the message on the mirror?" Jim was visibly angry.

"First the notes, and now this. You've got to get her some protection."

Victor held up one hand to ward off the fierce attack Jim was warming up to.

"I tried to call you this morning, but there was no answer."

"Jim and I went skiing. This is what we found when we returned." Her lip quivered a bit. "Why did you call?"

"We released Josef Ray yesterday."

"What!" Jim was livid.

"We had no choice. There was no substantial evidence to hold him. His handwriting wasn't even close to the writing on the note you received. He admitted to being at the psychic fair, and insists that he can identify the man if we can find him. He even offered to bring in the sample of the man's handwriting. I told him to do it. Maybe we'll know more then."

"Apparently he spent his morning systematically going through my things."

"Part of his morning you mean." Jim's brow was deeply furrowed.

"What's that?" Victor asked bluntly.

"Look, there was a ... incident on the ski slope."

"Jim, really, I think it was some careless skier out for a cheap thrill."

"Let him finish," Victor admonished, concern etched in every line of his face.

"I was higher up the slope; saw the whole thing. This guy—I assume it was a man—deliberately shoved Taylor onto a black run. Sanchez, she could have been killed. It's an extreme ski run, nearly straight down, lots of rocks, trees, and moguls. God, I tried to get to her but I was too far away."

"What happened?" Sanchez prompted.

"Saved herself. I couldn't believe it. She stabbed a straw bale with her pole and held on. Most amazing thing I ever saw."

"Are you hurt?"

"Just a sore arm, Victor. My wrist took a beating, and I think I'll probably have bruises, but otherwise I'm fine."

"So Sanchez," Jim said.

Taylor could not remember Jim ever calling Victor by his first name. She wished there was something she could do to ease the animosity between these two important men in her life.

"What are you going to do about this?"

"Let's sit down," Taylor said. "I'm ready to collapse." She fell into a stuffed, boxy chair—her favorite—covered in a textured white cotton weave. Victor took the closest end on the sofa and spread one arm along the back. Jim paced through the scattered newspapers on the floor.

After a few moments of uncomfortable silence, Sanchez leaned forward as if to soften the blow and addressed her reluctantly.

"Taylor, I'm afraid we have a stalker situation."

"That's crazy."

"No, not really. The notes and now the fondling of your things."

"That's disgusting. Fondling? What a terrible word."

"Exactly, but that's how he—or she—can feel closer to you. A stalker will often follow his victim to learn where she works or lives, and to establish when she will be out of her home or office. It's an obsession. The more they know about the victim, the more intimate the relationship—to the stalker, that is."

"I don't understand. Who'd want to stalk me?"

"Have you rejected anyone's manuscript lately who didn't take it well?"

"I thought the first note was from a writer. Now I'm not so sure. Course, that's always a clear and present danger," Taylor tried to joke. She felt sick.

"What made you change your mind about it being a writer?" Sanchez asked.

"Simple. No reference was ever made to writing. I think I preferred to believe that theory because I just could not fathom anything else."

"Something else we have to consider," Victor weighed his statement carefully, "Josef Ray may not be our man."

"Then who?" Taylor didn't want to recognize this even more frightening tidbit.

"It could be anyone," he said. "Someone who saw you giving a lecture; watched you on TV. Or took an interest in you, for whatever reason, when he encountered you on the street. It doesn't have to make sense. Not to a stalker. They disrupt a victim's work, day-to-day activities, and sometimes even force them into hiding. They ruin lives. The laws are relatively new. A conviction isn't easy. Most of the burden of proof lies with the victim."

Victor softened his voice. "I'm sorry, Taylor, but I think we have to look at all possibilities."

"Who's this?" Victor plucked Cheddar from the floor in one hand as he loudly demonstrated his need to be cuddled. He made an effective subject changer, providing comic relief to a tense situation. Victor curled him comfortably along his arm and scratched his head. The kitten immediately stopped shrieking and began an enthusiastic purr.

"That's the new one," Jim said. "Cheddar is a save. Taylor provides a cat rescue service when not editing mysteries or doing extreme skiing." Jim's sense of humor, for what it was, seemed to have returned.

"Why Cheddar?" Victor asked.

"I don't know." Taylor was still trying to digest the information he had offered. "I think because of his orange color. It seemed to fit."

Oscar leaped to Taylor's lap and settled in to bathe. Everything would be put to right. Taylor smoothed the fur where the string had been tied.

"Why the bells around Oscar's neck?"

"He probably wanted to emphasize how close he got and how much power he has."

"Vic," the officer named Sam interrupted. Two officers had spent the last quarter hour looking through the ruins of her house. "I've got prints but I think they'll prove to be the victim's." Taylor hated the repeated use of this term and itched to protest.

"Perp forced entry through the sliding glass doors. I'll get with you back at the station." He moved to go but said,

"Nice cat."

While Victor's mouth made nary a twitch though Taylor guessed it was all he could do to contain himself, much to his embarrassment. Cradling a kitten was not a macho thing to do.

"That will be all," Victor said sharply. Taylor saw the

officer's shoulders shake with laughter as he left by the front door.

"It might be a good idea to have someone nearby. Don't go out alone." Victor placed Cheddar on the floor and regained some of his authority. Cheddar was no longer a happy camper and meowed discontentedly.

"Is that all! You're just going to tell her not to go out alone. No cop to watch her?" Jim insisted. "I'll ask you again, what are you going to do about this?"

"Legally this is a break-in and will have to be treated as such." Victor stood and his face had warmed several degrees. To Taylor, "We can't do much about a stalker until we know who he is. Then you can file a police report and obtain a restraining order. Unfortunately, these usually aren't very effective because stalkers have lots of time to invest in their compulsion. Often they can be bright people capable of avoiding arrest. There are several types of stalkers. This guy could just be the nuisance variety. They want to be close and usually aren't dangerous. The dependent stalker also is not generally dangerous but is more persistent and frustrating. The dangerous types include the controller and the sadistic stalker. The controlling stalker normally has superficial social skills allowing him to move around in the mainstream population. The sadistic type deliberately creates fear in his victim and intends to commit violence from the inception."

He was standing near Jim by the time he finished. Intimidation?

"I've put a watch order on Taylor's house and we will continue to investigate."

Jim stepped sideways and picked up Cheddar. Taylor didn't know if it was to avoid Victor or because Cheddar was asking for attention.

"Place a board in the door track," Victor said. "Don't hesitate to call if you hear or see anything, *anything*, out of the ordinary. I mean that."

Taylor could tell he did. His face had softened dramatically when he turned to address her.

"Would you like me to stay?" Jim asked with concern. "We

could do the slumber party scene." Mockery was Jim's comfort zone.

"Thank you," she was not amused. "I'll be fine and I already have two roommates."

When everyone was gone, Taylor placed a board she cut to fit, in the track of the sliding door. No one would get in this way again. After securing the door, she cleaned the lipstick from her mirror. The handwriting analyst's card was in plain sight where she had left it after her visit to the police station. It should probably go back to Victor. But first, she had a use for it.

CHAPTER 8

After washing down a couple of aspirin, Taylor turned to wiping the intruder from her things. She triple-checked the locks and then shut Oscar and Cheddar in the spare bedroom, which had been untouched. Perhaps he hadn't had time or maybe it was because she didn't keep any personal things there. It served as a guest room and remained a basically generic space. But she wanted them safe while she cleaned.

Taylor filled the washing machine with as much of her clothing as it would hold and turned it on. By the time she went to bed everything would be washed, and the house thoroughly cleaned in spite of her aching body. Tomorrow she could rest.

With the washer going, Taylor started the laptop for a little research.

Josef Ray was not listed in the New Mexico white pages. Taylor wasn't surprised. The phone number on the handwriting analyst's card didn't draw a match in a city register, but a university directory check revealed he was an adjunct professor of English and listed as J. L. Ray at a west-side Santa Fe address. This surprised her. How many English teachers found work reading palms for a living? But without a full-time job, he probably had to do something else to survive. Taylor scribbled the address, checked for accuracy. The vacuuming would have to wait.

Taylor turned on Agua Fria at the Santuario de Guadalupe. That wasn't its official name but at the moment she couldn't recall the correct name. She thought it a long one. Agua Fria was a narrow, sometimes winding street that angled away from downtown in a southwesterly direction. After a few blocks she turned onto a side street. This neighborhood was a bit schizophrenic. Very neat houses were about evenly matched in number with those that had seen better days. They were mostly undersized with a few exceptions, the victims of grotesque remodeling. The lots did not allow for outward expansions so the occupants had built up, creating an unbalanced look. Several appeared about to topple from the top-heavy additions. Surprisingly, code enforcement—very strict in Santa Fe—had allowed the additions to stand.

Parked cars were everywhere, blocking the already cramped street. Children on tricycles skidded helter-skelter between cars and in and out of driveways in a dangerous fashion. A squashed red ball lay abandoned in the street where it had met its fate. Few residents had made an attempt at landscaping. Some yards consisted of nothing but white gravel. An occasional chamisa spread its plumage in disarray. A brave aging piñon stood damaged and taken for granted. One too many children had climbed its knobby arms.

Here lived native Santa Feans, those forgotten people who had not shared in Santa Fe's affluence. Most had suffered a decreased standard of living as the city attracted more well-heeled people to the big houses in the hills north of town. Tourism had provided jobs in the luxury hotel housekeeping departments and the restaurant service industry, but that was as close to the opulence as many of the natives would ever get. It was a wonder that they remained as kind and tolerant of visitors and newcomers as they were. Taylor had found most born and raised Santa Feans to be warm, friendly people in spite of the unequal distribution of wealth.

The address she was looking for turned out to be on a corner. She pulled over on the west side of the street because two cars were parked in front of the house. There were no double garages in the area. Second cars lived in the mean streets. She followed a well-worn path, a short cut for kids and dogs, across the corner of the property under a tree. The house was small, like the others, and was old enough to have been made of real adobe. The newer houses were not, they only looked the part. Most consisted of concrete blocks, and regular building materials, coated with stucco and painted brown.

The ramshackle portal was leaking melting snow onto the porch floor from the flat roof where it had collected. Several garbage bags rested against the wall, neatly tied, but a dog had torn into the bottom of one, dragging its contents across the yard. There was a patch of snow left in the shadow of the stucco wall. Water also dripped from the roof. It would be an icy mess by morning.

Taylor hesitated at the front door, a once bright turquoise wooden affair. The paint was peeling and some dry rot was affecting the bottom edge. It had once been a graceful arched entry. The door contained a formerly pretty leaded glass window, cracked with time and use. Now that she was here she wasn't certain how to proceed. Surely, if he'd been the same person who trashed her things, he would have taken his business card from the dresser where she left it. He could not have missed seeing it while ruining her favorite lipstick on the mirror. Even Victor had conceded that his handwriting did not match the notes she had received and that he was probably not the person who broke into her house. Something about him at the police station had seemed sincere to Taylor. He was frightened for himself, and, she felt, for her. With pounding heart she rang the doorbell. Nothing.

She looked through the fractured glass into the living room. The hardwood floor was badly scratched and marred but must have been beautiful once. A 1940s era blue couch was the only furniture, with the exception of a rough table holding a TV. The fabric on the couch was faded and threadbare. Stuffing exploded from one arm that had seen too many elbows. Although an antenna perched atop the house, the TV had rabbit ears—an ancient system! A frayed braided rug lay in the middle of the floor. The weaver's hard work had long ago been damaged. The remains lay on the dirty floor, seams pulled apart, braids unraveled. There was no sign of life. Having screwed up her courage to come this far, Taylor didn't want to leave. The door swung inward with only the slightest knock.

If, just if, Ray had been the one who broke into her house it would be only fitting that she return the favor. She knew this to be a gross rationalization, but crossed the threshold anyway.

"Hello," she called. "Anyone home?" There was the faint smell of burned coffee. "Hello?"

A mirror reflected an empty yard behind her and a very white face, her own. That nagging little inner voice was suggesting strongly that she leave. But it was only an empty house, nothing to be feared. Of course, breaking and entering could get you sent up the river. But Victor need never know about her indiscretion.

A short hall emptied to her left and led to a bedroom and bath. The bedclothes were still tangled from the last use. The air here smelled sour from dirty sheets and baskets of laundry. Taylor wrinkled her nose and checked the bathroom. The faucet had dripped for a long time. A rust stain spilled down the old pedestal sink where it had ruined the porcelain. There was no tub, only a timeworn shower. Taylor recoiled at the moldy tile and made a fast retreat to the dim hall. One picture adorned the filthy walls. A cheap reproduction of Jesus Christ praying, eyes cast upward to the light beams stretching heavenward. It had hung there long before Josef Ray dwelled within these walls.

The sink in the tiny kitchen was heaped with dirty dishes, the kind of crusty mess that lesser evolved creatures would inhabit. A periodic drip made rivulets in the fetid water that had been run to soak the pots and pans. The former contents were no longer recognizable. There was no coffee brewing, but the days-old glass pot sported fuzzy green yuck floating on the undrinkable brown liquid. Her shoe crunched a cracker still in the cellophane wrapper, a keepsake from a visit to a fast-food restaurant. The crunching was preferable to the sticky, obnoxious residue covering the floor. She drew the line at opening the refrigerator. It was likely to be another purveyor of penicillin.

A butler's pantry, barely more than an enclosed back porch, connected the kitchen with a dining room. The backyard was small and contained a rusty storage shed minus a door. A large dog bowl sat next to a coiled hose that had burst after repeated freezing temperatures. There was no sign of a dog.

The coffee smell was stronger here with a repulsive note. Taylor strained to hear. She didn't want to be surprised by an angry Josef Ray. He might even understand she thought, rationalizing once again. After all, he had seemed terribly concerned with her safety. The breakfront wedged into the cramped hall was the only piece of furniture there. It was stuffed with books about handwriting analysis, palm reading, dream interpretation, and other metaphysical topics. Stacks of papers contained a multitude of different handwriting. From appearances, Ray at least tried to be legit. A hat and ragged coat hung from hooks on the wall next to the back door.

Handsome woodwork in the dining room must have seen some festive dinners in its prime. It had remained fairly new looking with most of the bumps and scratches near the floor. Ray had set up his office here. A lone file cabinet stood next to her, head high. An old oak desk took up most of the floor space. It too, was heavy with accumulated books and papers. A torn blotter lay among the piles. It no longer held any paper and Taylor wondered why he'd keep it, especially with that huge coffee stain.

Except it wasn't coffee. Taylor could feel the scream rising from her soul. She clamped both hands over her mouth to stop it. Unfortunately, that left nothing to cover her eyes.

Josef Ray was dead. He was lying on top of a box of books, his knees bent, cowboy boots resting on the floor. The stringy hair was matted with blood that had splattered when he was stabbed. His emaciated body had received a deep wound. The worst offense was to his hands. Each of his slim, sensitive hands had been defaced. Taylor could stand no more; her lunch was coming up fast. She headed for the back door.

Within ten minutes the police were everywhere. Four patrol cars blocked the streets. An ambulance had been called but the attendants stood by, talking and laughing, waiting for the crime scene to be photographed.

Taylor cringed on the blue couch. After emptying her stomach on the back porch she had phoned the police. She'd had the wherewithal to remember not to touch anything. She wanted nothing more to do with the study so she had waited on the front step until the police arrived.

In a few minutes, Victor sauntered up to the house.

"What on earth are you doing here? No, no, wait, answer this. What was the last thing I asked you to do before I left your place?" He was furious. She thought he was also frightened, for her.

"You told me not to go anywhere alone." He had her red-handed. Technically, he had only suggested she not go out alone but this didn't seem the time to correct him.

"Not only did you disobey an order, but here you are at a crime scene. Taylor, don't you ever stay out of trouble?"

She stood in fury. "I'm not one of your lackeys!" Taylor shook her index finger savagely.

An officer standing behind Victor cleared his throat. The look on his young face suggested he knew what Taylor was going through.

"Detective Sanchez, I think you better take a look at the body. It appears someone tried to remove the ... uh, palms." Victor left the room in a huff.

"Ma'am, are you okay?" the officer asked. He didn't look old enough to be a policeman.

"I'm fine."

"Yes ma'am."

God, she felt wiped out.

Outside neighbors strained for a glimpse of violence, as if they didn't get enough on the nightly news. This kind of crime didn't happen every day in any neighborhood of Santa Fe. It was still a beautiful day, but the temperature had dropped a few degrees. They might get some snow tonight. The cool air helped to clear her head, which was throbbing above her right eye.

"Taylor." Victor had returned from the horror inside. His voice was still angry.

"What!" she answered testily.

"Look, I'm sorry about that, but we have something more important to discuss." She waited. "Do you know who that is?"

"Josef Ray."

"Right. It's possible he's been dead since yesterday, maybe right after we released him. Can't pinpoint it that closely though. It's likely he wasn't alive to push you down that slope today."

"You're saying?"

"We can't be sure if there is a connection between Ray's murder and the notes you've been receiving, but we can't take any chances either."

"So he wasn't lying. He wasn't the one."

"It doesn't look like it."

"Why did the killer ... disfigure his hands?" She could barely get the words out.

"I could only speculate at this point; probably something to do with him being a handwriting analyst."

"Was he ... tortured?" For some reason Taylor felt responsible.

"Don't know that either. Could have been done after he was killed." He motioned to the rookie officer.

"Please escort Ms. Browning home."

"I drove."

"He'll follow you home; make sure your house is secure."

She longed to have someone hold her, tell her everything was okay.

"Victor, I'm sorry about that."

"No problem, I've heard worse. Go home."

So here they were again; square one. Victor telling her to go home. It had been a stupid thing to do. A mistake she hoped never to repeat.

CHAPTER 9

Victor was beat. He hung his jacket from a hook next to the back door of his south side house. It was close to the station but he and his wife had bought in this location because it was affordable for a young family. The three-bedroom, two-bath house was too big for him now. It was nights like this that he especially missed his wife and daughter, killed by a drunk driver several years ago.

He'd set up his office in the dining room because he couldn't spend any time in either his daughter's room or the master bedroom. Even after he'd sold the furniture and given away their clothes he couldn't use the rooms. He slept in the guest room and kept the other doors closed. His sister was probably right. He should sell the house, yet he remained with his memories.

Victor looked out the glass doors of the kitchen eating area to the backyard that he no longer tended. When his wife had been alive she nurtured the trees and shrubs. In the summer she had grown flowers and a vegetable garden. Some of those flowers had come up by themselves last summer, self-seeded, but they had been tangled with grass and weeds. Finally the flowers died, choked by the stronger weeds; a sad remembrance. His sister had given away the swing set right after the funeral. It had been his daughter's. At the time he could not bear to see it.

If he wasn't working, he was a lonely man. There was no one to talk with or focus his attention on, not a dog, not even a plant.

For a moment he thought of Taylor and her two cats. She'd made a family, someone to love, two creatures who depended on her. His work took so much time, his fault by his own admission, but he had no other family in Santa Fe and most of his friends were from the force. Except of course, for Taylor. He wasn't sure he'd be counted among her friends at the present moment after the verbal beating she'd taken from him earlier. Certainly, she had given it right back—an admirable trait, however annoying. He was accustomed to fearful respect and she obviously was not frightened of him. Unfortunately, she didn't seem to be frightened of much.

He pulled a frozen dinner from the freezer and stuffed it into the microwave. While another luscious meal was assaulted with microwaves he dumped the remainder of the morning's coffee and started a fresh pot.

To say he was baffled by the apparent stalker would be an understatement. Why would anyone stalk Taylor? Somehow the angry writer theory didn't wash. He would, however, have her give him any letters of this type for careful scrutiny.

With two unsolved murders he was frustrated. Still nothing on the woman killed in the parking garage a little over a week ago. She had worked at the hotel across the street doing housekeeping. This was strange in itself because the personnel director at the hotel told him she was a college graduate qualified for better paying jobs. Apparently he had offered her a position in administration but she had insisted on the housekeeping job.

Linda Smith Adams had grown up in Oregon and had earned a degree in business from the Oregon State University in Corvallis. She landed a great job in Portland where she met her husband. The information from the Portland PD showed that a protective order had been filed against her husband, Gary Adams. She'd made repeated trips to court in a vain attempt to enforce the order. Her attorney told Victor by phone the victim had been terrified of her ex-husband and pleaded with the judge to do something. Apparently, Linda Adams had fled Oregon to escape her husband. He was the prime suspect at the moment in her murder but no evidence had been found to directly connect him to the crime. In fact, he was nowhere to be found.

Gary Adams' degree in marketing had landed him a good position as an advertising executive in one of Portland's biggest firms. He'd made a six-figure income and had been promoted to vice president when his wife pressed charges for assault and battery. That was the end of his career with the prestigious company. After that he worked at a couple of small advertising companies but his temper and confrontational attitude become more and more volatile as his career plummeted. It was bad enough at work, where he was prone to tantrums that turned to torrents of expletives and flying office furniture, but horrendous for his wife who suffered for his perceived slights in a world where he increasingly couldn't cope.

Earlier court records had disclosed a troubled youth, beginning with complaints from neighbors concerning cruelty to animals and missing pets. He'd spent some time in a boys' home after being convicted of several burglaries and car theft.

With his parents' considerable money he attended an Eastern prep school and graduated with honors. Despite being a bright boy, there had been problems in school. What these had been was not clear. Victor felt the Adam's money had been sufficient to hush up these incidents. The report suggested that assault and battery had once again been his crime. These accounts were not substantiated, however, but were included because several women at the university had made complaints, only to withdraw them. Because they wished to remain anonymous and did not press charges, he had escaped prosecution, and since his juvenile offenses had been ameliorated, his record remained clean.

Adams had managed to convince the authorities of his reformation by leading an exemplary life while confined. Victor couldn't discount other possibilities for Linda Adams murder, but her residency in Santa Fe had been only two months, hardly enough to draw from. She had few friends, they didn't know her well, and she had lived a very quiet, private life, hiding from her ex-husband.

The timer beeped at him and he turned the plastic tray a half-turn, reset it, and poured a cup of the steaming coffee. It was too strong. He'd never been able to duplicate his wife's coffee-making skills. Even that swill at work was better than he could do. He drank it anyway.

The latest crime was particularly gruesome. Josef Ray had been more than murdered; the stab wound, was deeper than necessary to kill him. Whoever did him in was angry. Victor had worked with the Albuquerque police force for several years and hadn't seen anything like this since moving back to Santa Fe nearly a decade ago. Even then, there had been only a few murders that weren't straightforward. The gang killings drove him to move to a quieter city.

If only he'd taken Josef Ray more seriously. He thought that Ray was blowing smoke to cover his own tracks. Still, there had been no solid evidence anyone else was involved, including Taylor's account of what happened at the psychic fair. With his background of petty crimes, there was every reason to believe he was trying to avoid yet another run-in with the police. Victor wished he'd gone with Ray to his home and looked at the writing sample. There were stacks of samples in his house and no way to determine the one he talked about. The department's handwriting analyst was busy going through the hundreds looking for those with the characteristics Ray had described. Victor didn't hold out much hope.

The TV dinner was turkey. He hated turkey; must have been left over from Thanksgiving. He sat alone at the breakfast table. The only light filtered through the shutters covering the pass-through to the dining room. His agitation prevented him from eating the full meal. The remainder would meet its demise in the disposal.

He picked up his cell phone from the table, dialed Taylor's number and waited for her familiar voice.

"This is Victor. Are we still speaking?"

"Barely." It was spoken with minor warmth.

"About those letters from writers. You know the ones angry about being rejected."

"I know the ones."

"Can you get them together? I'd like to have our handwriting expert take a look at them. Might even send them to a lab in Albuquerque."

"I still have them at work. I'll get them."

"Thanks. And Taylor?" She waited quietly. "I'm sorry I got so bent out of shape today. I ... care about you. Okay?"

"Okay." She hung up. Still peeved.

Taylor replaced the receiver. She sat in her home office and considered Victor's comments. He cared about her. Well, she hadn't much appreciated the way he had demonstrated that today. He had telephoned, but only to ask for those stupid letters. Maybe, just maybe, that was his excuse. Why he needed one Taylor had no idea.

She spent her evening cleaning house, trying to erase every touch of the intruder. The place reeked of lemon-fresh environmentally friendly furniture polish. Her office was the only room remaining to be put right. The office had been a spontaneous decision for Taylor. Originally, she'd wanted to build one off the back of the house under the aspen. During a conversation with Jim he mentioned there wasn't much she could do with the L-shaped living room and the area near the front door was rarely used. He offered the services of a friend and carpenter. A week later she had two new walls and an office. It was small, about ten by ten feet, but perfect for her. The large window allowed a fine view of the lilac hedge along her drive and the chamisa dotted front yard. She added a birdbath and feeder for her entertainment while taking breaks from editing chores. Next spring she would add flowers.

As was her nature, she'd moved right in, without finishing the walls—an idiosyncrasy that was becoming well established. The beige laminated office furniture was purchased locally. Jim had helped her assemble the large desk. Her computer was much more convenient now. It had been kept in the spare bedroom on a rickety old typewriter table. She used it mostly for editing purposes and the home office provided a quiet respite from her work environment that could be quite frenzied at times. When she wore her promotions hat, her office at Piñon Publishing was perfect, but like Virginia, she found editing to be more productive in relative peace and quiet.

Except for her office, everything seemed to be back in place, but Taylor wished there was some way to eradicate every trace of the person who had violated her home, plundered her things, and frightened her cats.

It was late, but she feared sleep would be a long time coming. She couldn't believe that in one day she had been pushed down a mountainside, only to return to the presumed safety and security of her home to find that illusion destroyed. In anger at the person who had done this, and at Victor for his inability to make it right, she had gone off half-cocked and discovered the brutalized body of a man who might have tried to help her. The vivid, horrifying recollection of that poor man dead in that shabby house would last forever. Sadly, any knowledge he may have had of the stalker died with him.

CHAPTER 10

Taylor thought seriously about staying home the next day but concluded it was better to go to work rather than obsess about the break-in. Normal activity was probably better for her. She had played hooky yesterday. Of course it was Jim's fault, but that was a little detail no one else would be interested in. There were three inches of new snow and the city glistened with freshness in the sunshine. The adobe houses displayed rounded white humps of the sparkling white along every rooftop, portal, and wall. The chamisa bent under the weight of the snow that covered the brown spent blooms of autumn, and hunter green piñon provided conspicuous contrast with the white earth. The redolent odor of piñon smoke enticed her to roll down her window a few inches so she could enjoy its distinctive fragrance. Vivaldi's *Four Seasons* played on the radio, not her favorite classical piece, but it seemed appropriate this pristine morning.

She had barely gotten settled at her desk when Jim buzzed her and ask her to join him in the freelancer's office.

Jim was talking with a man Taylor thought familiar but she couldn't quite remember where she knew him.

"Taylor, this is Eric Powers. He's going to be working with us on the cover of *Spirit, Mind & Bodies.*"

"How do you do. I'm Taylor Browning." She offered her hand and he took it in one of his fine, delicate ones.

"We met briefly the other morning." His smile warmed the room. "How nice to make it official."

She remembered. He was the man Candi had been drooling over. Taylor had to agree with her, he was quite a divine being. Eric Powers was deeply tanned, odd for this time of year, but maybe he'd been skiing. He wore an unconstructed navy suit, rough silk and very expensive, with a deep purple T-shirt. The effect was coastal. Only his hair spoiled an otherwise perfect facade. It was colored and looked unnatural. Taylor surmised that he had a few greys and wanted to cover them. What a shame.

"Are you new to Santa Fe?" Taylor asked.

"Yes, I'm from the east coast."

"New Mexico must be a bit of a culture shock for you."

"A pleasant one. I'm looking forward to the opera next summer and in the meantime, I plan on doing a lot of fly-fishing and hiking. As near as I can tell, New Mexico has everything." Taylor almost smiled with approval. She didn't care for people who belittled one area of the country over another. Every region had its own wonders. Eric was saying all the right things.

"I thought," Jim interrupted her reflection. "We needed a different look for the Crystal Visions book—something with graphic layering rather than the usual vector images most of our mysteries sport. When Eric dropped off his resume the other morning I noticed he had a great deal of experience in this area. He already has a sample cover to show us."

"Did you give him a copy of the synopsis?" Taylor asked.

"Oh, yes," Eric smiled. "A most unusual book by mystery standards." He removed a prototype from his briefcase and laid it on the light box. Jim flipped the switch that backlit the glass top.

"The background is a deep, rich rusty red—the color of the red rocks of Sedona," Eric said. "I understand the author lives there and, of course, the action takes place in that area." He smoothed the sample cover lovingly.

A bright white light burst from the top left corner, and a

circle of rocks took center stage, a yellow candle burned with-in. There was a smear of blood on two of the stones.

"The circle of rocks is the method used to mark the location of a vortex. The candle is suggestive of meditation," he explained. "Of course, the blood alludes to the mystery."

"The font will be black. Should pop nicely off the cover."

"Do you use Adobe?" Jim asked, referring to one of the software systems used to make camera-ready art.

"Yes, the Creative Suite."

"I like it," Taylor complimented Eric Power's work in a voice a bit too sweet. "Don't you?" she asked Jim and didn't let him answer. "May I have a color copy to send to the author?"

"Sure," Eric agreed.

Jim was a bit surprised by Taylor's honeyed inflection. Was she flirting? This was a first. He'd never known her to behave in this manner, certainly not with him. It was irksome.

Taylor studied Eric for a moment. He was discussing the finer elements of style with Jim and neither seemed to notice her presence. She thought he might be a great addition to the office and hoped he would be around a lot. Not only was he easy on the eyes, but his work was competent. The office could use some more proficiency. With Jessica's outbursts, fueled by inexperience and indecision, it was difficult to get through a day without some sort of commotion. Freelancers or employees who demonstrated knowledge of their craft were most welcome.

"Jim?" It was Penny. "Oh, here you are." She batted long lashes and quickly sized up Eric. He was a bit more discreet in his observations. Jim made introductions and she spewed forth adulation over the cover. Taylor felt ill and bit chagrined. Jim was standing against the wall watching it all play out, highly amused.

"Taylor! I've been looking all over for you." Jessica burst in the room, which was growing smaller with each additional human. Her presence consumed what was left. Attired in a bright purple business suit made expressly to fit her voluptuous figure, Jessica, as usual, made a lasting impression. She, herself, confessed to coloring her hair *hooker red*. An orange silk scarf was fitted around her porcelain neck, setting off an ample chest that heaved wildly when she was provoked. It was heaving now.

"I'm right here," Taylor said certain that Jessica was exaggerating.

"Have you heard from *her* yet?"

After Taylor had saved Jessica's life, they had shared a kind of bond for a while, but as Jessica became more and more dumbfounded with the business she had inherited, she had distanced herself from everyone, even those who could help her the most.

"Which *her* would that be?" Taylor asked with just a touch of reproach.

"Who else is late with a manuscript?" She eyed Taylor dangerously. She hadn't missed the censure in Taylor's voice. Jessica didn't miss much along those lines. Her instincts in matters of disapproval were finely honed from years of suffering at the hands of her ex-husband.

"No, still nothing from Crystal. Candi keeps trying. I've tried."

"Do *you* need to be here?" Jessica demanded of Penny. "Don't you have some spread-sheets to look at? If you're short on work I'm sure our senior editor can find you some pencils to sharpen."

Penny's eyes blazed, but she departed swiftly.

"Try her again. If she doesn't make contact I want you to go out there!"

"To Sedona?" Taylor said, taken aback.

"Yes. Find that blasted woman and take the manuscript by force if you have to."

This to Eric, "Who are you?" She gave him a none too subtle once over.

"Jessica, this is Eric Powers," Jim said. "He's working with me on the cover of Crystal Vision's book. He specializes in graphic design."

"You're hiring now too?" Her carefully penciled brows arched dramatically.

"Jessica." Taylor recognized Jim was reaching the outer

limits of his patience, something he wasn't known for anyway. "He's a freelancer, working on this book only. Would you like to see his prototype?"

She gave it a perfunctory glance.

"That's fine." Jessica knew next to nothing about book covers, what made a frontlist book or midlist book, what the font size of an author's name meant, or how it could be used to market the book to bestseller status.

"You might keep in mind, uh, Eric, that if we don't get the manuscript your assignment will be quite brief. Jessica flounced out, leaving enough electricity in the room to light a bulb.

"Interesting woman," Eric replied noncommittally.

"Sedona?" Taylor said puzzled. "She wants me to go to Arizona to get a manuscript? What about the book I'm supposed to have edited next week? What about the promotions on our new books? A trip at this time doesn't make sense."

"Sense?" Jim said. "I wish our new leader had some." He quickly looked to the door to see if Jessica had overheard his remark. There was no sign of her.

"Witch." Penny Lane sat in her office and quietly cursed Jessica. She missed Massachusetts. It was nothing like this dry, godforsaken land. She'd taken this job because she was angry with her parents. They wished for her to get married and live happily ever after in Boston. She wanted to pursue a career with the degree she had worked hard to obtain. Although her parents had a great deal of money, it didn't buy her grades, just one of the best educations available. She liked Virginia Compton, who called her university for referrals. Penny had moved, at her own expense, halfway across the country to take what sounded like a promising job, only to find herself caught in the middle of two quarreling women. Apparently, there was some kind of hostility between Virginia and Jessica, and she was taking the brunt of it. Whatever, she had not been given a chance to show her stuff since Jessica had discovered she was here. It was very unfair to her.

Jim had been nice to her, even solicitous, but he couldn't make her life any more pleasant. That had to come from

Virginia and Jessica. She'd give this poor excuse for a business a couple more weeks and if things didn't shape up she'd leave right before Christmas—and right before tax time. That would give the red-haired biddy reason to be upset.

Taylor sealed the Express Mail envelope with resolve. It was settled. If Crystal did not respond to this she was to go to Sedona. Taylor had never been to Arizona, so the idea of seeing some new country appealed, but dealing with Crystal most certainly did not.

"Excuse me, ma'am." It was the young officer she'd met at Josef Ray's house. "I'm officer Matt Chambers. I'm supposed to pick up some letters."

"Oh, yes. They're here." Taylor handed the white envelope containing three letters from irate authors. Two were unsigned; the other was from a man in Taos.

He took the envelope. "Are you doing okay?" He hesitated. "After your ... ordeal."

"Yes, thank you. I'm getting quite used to finding bodies. It seems to be a long undeveloped talent that has come out of dormancy since my arrival in Santa Fe." The poor guy looked confused and why wouldn't he?

"But, I appreciate your asking." She smiled.

"Have a nice day, ma'am."

"And don't call me ma'am," she said to no one a few moments later. "It makes me feel old."

Taylor had the beginnings of a headache and rubbed her temples gingerly. She carried the envelope for Crystal to Alise's desk. She was nowhere to be seen. No surprise there. When Jessica was gone you could bet on Alise disappearing too, most likely reading a romance novel in Jessica's office, feet on her desk. Taylor resisted the urge to open Jessica's door.

"Might as well take it myself. Then I guess I'll go home and pack." She was certain Crystal Visions would respond to this communiqué as she had to the others—not at all.

CHAPTER 11

"Don't worry about Oscar and Cheddar," Jim was saying as he unloaded Taylor's black bag from his Jeep and placed it on the sidewalk outside the Albuquerque International Sunport in line for a sky cap. As usual Jim was late, and now she didn't have time to check in at the ticket counter.

"I solemnly promise to feed them twice a day, separately," his hand raised in pledge. "I will even pet them."

"I'm concerned about leaving them at home since the break-in." Taylor ignored him. "Maybe I should have boarded them at the vet."

"You know what Sanchez said," Jim tried for reassurance. "As long as you're gone it's not likely the stalker will bother your house again. If you recall you said he thought it was a good idea for you to leave town for a while."

"Still."

"Look," Jim touched her shoulder, "if it will make you feel better I'll go by at lunch too."

"Oh, Jim, would you?"

"Taylor, dear, have I ever denied you anything?"

"Come on Jim." She punched his arm in a sophomoric gesture. "Just when I think you're a real person you say something like that." His only answer was a dazzling smile. She could really love-hate him sometimes.

"What's your flight number?" The skycap asked Taylor when they had finally scuffled to the head of the line.

She handed him her boarding pass. He took her bag and tied a tag with the city code PHX to its handle. "Concourse A," he said.

"You better get going," Jim said. "Hope you ate something."

"I haven't. I'll gorge myself on peanuts."

"Here's an apple." Jim tossed her a Granny Smith. She stuffed it into her bulging handbag.

"Jim."

"Yes, luv?"

"If there are any problems, please take the cats to my vet. The number's next to the kitchen phone."

"Don't worry. I'll will move into your house or take them to mine. Have fun in the twilight zone," he made reference to Sedona's reputation as a New Age center. Jim blew her a kiss, slammed the door of the Jeep, and roared off.

"Very funny." At least Taylor hoped so.

Was there anything worse than being left alone at an airport? Taylor felt sad and vulnerable. She wished Jim hadn't returned in a hurry, but work called.

Taylor had seen photos of the *old* airport; it had been full of character and charm with narrow gate areas and ochre Mexican tile. It had been a truly unique facility, in keeping with the architecture and landscape of New Mexico. The flip side was an extremely inefficient airport with long waits for luggage and concourses packed like sardines. The renovations had produced wide, roomy common areas in adobe brown accented with blue. The beautiful original viga ceiling was saved from demolition and was a delight to view while nothing else occupied her on the escalator. The massive beams overhead reached far across the common area. High windows illuminated roadrunners, rabbits, and other characters where they were notched, carved, and painted in pale desert colors along the smooth timbers. As airports go, it was attractive. Although designers had made the effort to retain some of the charm it looked much like other city airports, albeit much more practical than before. A major goof was the seating at the gates. The

Mexican style chairs in blocky wood with thin vinyl strips, an attempt at retaining character, had been grossly uncomfortable and were soon replaced with more comfortable padded seats.

She looked wistfully out the huge windows along the concourse at a cloudless azure sky just touched with haze. In Albuquerque, residents could burn their fireplaces only on designated nights because of the growing smog problem. The valley collected and held the smoke, leaving the city no choice except to specify no-burn days.

Taylor pulled out the malachite stone from her purse. She decided to carry it for its supposed protective quality. The psychic fair had rubbed off on her. Maybe it was nothing, but just having it with her made her feel safer.

A couple hours later, Albuquerque remained miles behind and Taylor craned to see as much of Phoenix as possible through the small oval window as the plane taxied to Sky Harbor. The desert city was very modern looking. Some of the skyline reminded her of Dallas' glass buildings reflecting in the sun. Most of what Taylor could see looked relatively new, having been built after the Age of Skyscrapers. And here in the Valley of the Sun was ample space. Buildings could go out rather than up and cost less money.

By the time she had rented an SUV—a red, not white, the color most rentals seem to be—her luggage had arrived. Fifteen minutes later she eased out of the rental car garage into the traffic. Interstate 17 steered north and she drove out of the warm city towards the mountains. When the traffic eased Taylor located a classical station and settled in for the drive. Outside the city limits the highway carved through a saguaro forest. The giant cactus seemed to wave as she drove past. How she wished for time to pull off and study them up close. Perhaps another time. This was an assignment. Her job was to find Crystal Visions and take possession of the manuscript.

The interstate gained altitude steadily as the SUV sped through the beautiful desert countryside. The runaway truck ramps made her a bit nervous. There were signs instructing drivers to shut off air conditioning while driving this portion of the trip due to the highway grade. Had it been summer, she would have been reluctant to shut off the cool, but today at the higher elevation the breeze through the window was quite comfortable for the few miles of grade.

Taylor mused about what to do if the book was not done. Was she to sit on Crystal and make her finish? Would a whip and chair be needed? Taylor thought an attorney might be more appropriate. Oh well, it was not for her to reason why; this was Jessica's game.

At Highway 179 she was relieved that the two-hour trip was nearly complete. This was the last leg, a fifteen-mile stretch to Sedona, which meandered through hills and passed through the Village of Oak Creek where the red rocks suddenly dominated. Bell Rock was easily identifiable. Taylor read several brochures on the plane and thought it odd that with all the Native American heritage of the area, the rocks were given names such as Coffee Pot and Snoopy Rock. Now seeing the individual formations, she could readily identify them from their names.

The beauty of the area was not easily described. The monolithic rocks were deep rust red and towered, sans trees, above Sedona which huddled below dwarfed by the formations. The canyon produced evergreen trees, shrubs, agave, and a version of prickly pear cactus known as cow's tongue, which bore an amazing resemblance to its namesake. The divergence was spectacular.

Taylor knew Crystal lived near Boynton Canyon, but had no idea where it was. At the intersection of Highway 89A, she turned into a small shopping center and asked for directions. The canyon was west of town on the highway to Jerome. She took Dry Creek Road as instructed and drove the road nearly three miles. After that she followed the signs. Boynton Canyon was a popular place.

A gatehouse loomed ahead. Crystal obviously lived in swanky parts. The gatekeeper, complete with shotgun, let her pass only after she showed him her card. He knew Crystal was an author.

The houses in this development were built for one-percenters. They were mostly white stucco with heavy red clay tile roofs. Many were two-story, three-car garage homes in excess of five thousand square feet. A few of the homes were constructed in the adobe style so popular in Santa Fe.

Taylor located Crystal's house and parked in the ample drive. The three-car garage angled away from the main house. She hesitated for a moment to catch her breath. It had taken nearly three hours to get here and she was tired. In addition, she wasn't sure how to approach Crystal. The author probably wasn't one for surprises, unless she pulled one herself. Taylor expected she would be miffed.

The flagstone walk from the garage to the front door was enclosed by a long, walled courtyard on the outside and the front wall of the house on the other. Tall stick-like plants called ocotillo and clumps of prickly pear grew along both sides of the path. Sword-leafed agave burst from drifting grounded sedum at their feet. The bluish hen and chicks had seen better days before a recent freeze that had left them wilted. Taylor imagined that brilliant purple verbenas, yellow desert marigold, and multicolor portulaca would dazzle the eye during warmer months.

The front door was sheltered by a pretentious two-story columned entry. Above the double doors was an arched window. Bay windows opened rooms to sunshine on either side of the heavy front doors. Taylor braced herself and rang the doorbell.

Several minutes later an older woman answered her ring. "Yes?"

"I'm Taylor Browning, here to see Crystal Visions. I'm from Piñon Publishing in Santa Fe."

"Is she expecting you?" she asked in broken English.

Was she? After numerous calls and letters Taylor probably would not be a complete surprise, but then again ...

"I'm not sure, but correspondence has been sent." That seemed safe.

"Please come in. I'll see if she is available." Taylor handed her the same card the gatekeeper had rumpled.

The foyer was protected by a great expanse of glass overhead that formed a cathedral ceiling. A formal dining room was on her right. Across the hall was a room that appeared to be Crystal's office. The house only looked multilevel. A long clerestory ran almost the full length of the house. Saltillo tile, at least a foot square each, sheathed the foyer floor and stretched into the living room across the columned hall. The fireplace was the focal point of the room and meant to be impressive. It was at least three metres wide. She was about to step across the hall when shuffling feet alerted her of an approach by humans.

"Why are you here?" Crystal demanded. The maid beat a hasty retreat. Today's head-to-toe turban look was navy. A red silk scarf cinched her tiny waist. Small red ballet slippers protruded from the long skirt. Crystal's black hair was pulled tightly back, caught with colorful paisley scarf and hung in a long silken pony tail from the nape of her neck. Exaggerated makeup only made her look more exotic. She had a wide face with the sculptured look of a model. Her large eyes practically entered the room before the rest of her. She wore pale blue eye shadow, the one normally reserved for blondes of questionable career, but on her dark skin it was stunning. A chunky necklace made of different types of wood hung nearly to her waist along with several strands of gold. Baubles adorned her hands in clattering splendor.

"Hello, Crystal. Nice to see you again." Taylor ignored her hostile greeting. "We haven't received an answer to any of our phone calls or letters so Jessica Endicott sent me to check on you."

"Who is Jessica Endicott?"

"The owner of Piñon Publishing."

"Oh, yes. Red hair."

Everyone remembered Jessica from her hair. "That's right.

"What do you want?"

"Simply, we need the complete manuscript for *Spirit, Mind & Bodies*."

"It's not ready yet. You go back and tell her that. You can't hurry creativity."

How many times had she heard that from cantankerous writers? Writers seem to come in three standard personalities: real people, dependable but strange, and disagreeable. Pretty much like people who don't write.

"Crystal," Taylor took a firm hand, "I will not go back without the manuscript. I have a copy of your signed contract with me stating the due date for the manuscript. If this was not satisfactory you should not have signed it, or requested another deadline. If it is necessary to contact our attorney, then I will. Now, if you will kindly recommend a hotel, I'll go get some much needed rest. It was a long drive. Tomorrow we'll get to work."

Several emotions flashed across Crystal's beautiful face. Taylor recognized anger and repressed the desire to duck. Had she seen uncertainty? The wheels turned behind those expressive eyes. Taylor suspected she was about to be thrown out bodily.

Instead. "Consuela!"

The lovely woman materialized very quickly. Taylor wondered if she had been listening nearby.

"Yes, ma'am." There was a touch of resentment in her voice.

"Please show Ms. Browning to the guest wing."

"Crystal, thank you, but that's not necessary," Taylor objected. She wasn't sure she wanted to stay here.

"Nonsense, I have four guest rooms. Besides, there is a convergence seminar going on. You probably could not get a room."

"I see. Thanks." Taylor didn't know how grateful to be. She felt as if she were staying in the wrong camp.

"This way please," Consuela indicated.

By the time Taylor turned back to Crystal she was padding her way silently down the long hallway, pony tail swinging with what? Fury?

"Does madam prefer a bath or shower?"

"Please call me Taylor, and a bath would be great."

"Yes, ma'am." Consuela led her through the hall in the opposite direction. The dining room was open on this side and the arch revealed an elegant space. It was most decidedly not southwestern. A gleaming dark walnut table sat precisely in the middle of the room. Ten traditionally crafted chairs with tapestry covered seats were placed evenly along the perimeter. A matching sideboard hugged the only unbroken wall. A crystal chandelier hung in dripping splendor. An unadorned bay window and brass sconces would provide soft light during an evening meal. Several pieces of art hung on two walls. Taylor did not know the artists and suspected they were local.

"The kitchen is here at the back of the house." Consuela waved at a small closed door. "I serve dinner in the dining room promptly at seven, breakfast also at seven in the morning room. Madam doesn't often eat lunch." Consuela had obviously been directed to speak formally. What a shame because Taylor thought she had a melodious voice that strained at propriety.

They turned down another hall, passing two doors with more arched entries and a circular staircase. "The first two bedrooms have showers," Consuela said as she passed the closed entrances.

"Where does that go?" Taylor asked about the spiral staircase.

"To a storage area," she replied succinctly.

It reminded Taylor of Mary Roberts Rinehart's, *The Circular Staircase*, and a chill darted through her body.

Past the eerie staircase, a small alcove contained an upholstered chair and table with landline. A *nicho* above the table held a collection of Native pots in tiny sizes. One was barely larger than a thimble.

"I think you'll be comfortable in the front bedroom—it is the largest and has a view of the courtyard. There's room in the garage if you would like to park your car there. An entrance to this wing from the garage is down the hall past the laundry facility. Let me know if you need anything." This must have amounted to a speech from Consuela No-Last-Name. She left abruptly.

As bedrooms go, it was large. A queen bed with bleached oak headboard and hand-painted detail was indisputably made by a craftsman. The fluffy comforter in sand and red flame stitch covered the bed. Under her feet, pale brown tiles were strewn with several Native American area rugs. Taylor wondered if they were Navajo. Near the large window was a desk with a phone. An overstuffed chair sat in the corner, along with a hassock for tired feet, and a floor lamp, made a perfect reading spot. The bathroom carried on the same theme but the walls carried accents in hunter green triangle shaped tiles that charged around the room at chest height. The Jacuzzi bathtub and the other fixtures contrasted in deep crimson.

Taylor washed her hands of travel grime and looked at the front columns from the small bathroom window. She felt a bit worn and uneasy from traveling all day. Staying with Crystal had been unexpected. She couldn't help but think again how much Crystal resembled the murdered Dominique Boucher. It gave her the willies.

CHAPTER 12

It was late in the day and Jim was trying to wrap things up so he could go home. First he would check on his feline charges, then unwind in his favorite chair—maybe watch some ESPN. His stack of messages was set aside with every intention of indefinitely postponing reading them.He was just rising from his chair when Jessica shrieked something about a file. This was not good. Her outbreaks were becoming increasingly frequent and more vitriolic. He was getting some idea of what her marriage to the former owner of Piñon Publishing must have been like. He'd thought Endicott was a tough nut, but his warmer feelings for Jessica were cooling.

What to do? He could sit quietly and maybe no one would notice him or it might be possible to sneak down the stairs and out of the office before things got too flammable. While he struggled with the best scenario, Jessica screamed his name. That ended any hope of escape.

"Jim!" she shouted again. "Come here. Help me find this blasted file."

Jim followed the vibrating walls to Taylor's office where Jessica stood among what were Taylor's meticulous editorial files. The drawer was open. Half a dozen files lay in chaos on the floor, one in danger of being impaled by Jessica's stiletto heel.

"Trouble, Jessica?"

Taylor was not going to be amused. She wasn't fussy about her desk, which always had stacks of manuscripts and other even more useless stuff all over it, but her files were kept so that anyone in the office could find something if needed; anyone but Jessica, apparently.

"I must have that file," she seethed.

"What file?" Jim was becoming angry. He'd probably have to straighten the mess if he couldn't enact some damage control.

"That New Age hussy."

"Have you looked under V?" Jim did not want to get any closer. Jessica had been known to throw things. "Under Visions."

"Don't get smart with me!" Her eyes sharpened as she attempted to make Jim slink.

"Jessica." Tiredly. "It's late. Can we just look for it tomorrow?"

"No! I need it now."

Jim approached the file cabinet, keeping as much distance between him and Jessica as possible in such small quarters.

"It's probably in the lower drawer." He closed the top one with a shove and gingerly extracted the Crystal Visions file and handed it to Jessica. He bent to pick up the scattered folders on the floor, carefully replacing the contents of each. Taylor was going to be ticked off. He'd no sooner gotten them collected when he was showered with paper.

"Idiot!" Jessica was viciously tearing Crystal's contract and photo into pieces. "I'll show you."

"What the ... ? Jessica! Geez, what are you doing?"

"Writers! Who does she think she is? I don't have to take this!" The tirade went on while Jim watched dumbfounded at the spectacle. In only a few minutes the complete file including all correspondence, synopsis, author photo, and completed chapters covered the office floor.

"Why haven't I heard from that girl?" Jessica demanded.

Jessica rarely called anyone by name. She either couldn't remember them or didn't bother.

"Taylor," he emphasized her name. "Taylor just left this

morning for Arizona on your order. She probably hasn't reached Crystal's house yet. Why don't we give her at least until tomorrow to report in?"

"Humph," Jessica snorted. "I suppose we'll have to but I won't be here. I'm leaving for LA immediately," she stated with returning calm. She marched to her office where she picked up her purse and left the office.

Virginia and Alise gathered outside Taylor's office. Alise was wide-eyed and flushed with excitement. Virginia coolly took in the scene.

"Son of a gun!" Jim said. "Would you look at this?" He rocked back on his heels and surveyed the spoils. "Taylor is going to be livid. What got into that woman?" He looked to Virginia for explanation but got none.

"Everything okay?" Candi joined them and shook her head in disbelief. "Jessica?"

"Bingo," Jim said. "Anyone care to assist in the cleanup?" Candi and Alise sat cross-legged on the floor and tried to salvage what they could. Jim replaced the other folders. Virginia left quietly. She would not be a part of cleaning up after *that* woman. Jessica could throw all the fits she wanted.

*   *   *

By seven Taylor had showered and changed from jeans and turtleneck to her favorite charcoal canvas skirt and a deep purple cable knit sweater. She pulled on black tights and slipped her feet into tasseled loafers. From across the room the telephone seemed to invite her to use it. On impulse she dialed her home number, charging it to her credit card. She was surprised when Jim answered almost immediately.

"Taylor, did you forget your cell? You haven't fallen into a vortex yet?"

"No, I didn't forget my cell. I wanted a good connection. Jim, what are you doing at my house at this time of evening? And no, I've managed to avoid being sucked into any vortexes."

"And, purely out of curiosity, why are you calling your empty house?"

"I thought, well ... " Taylor was reluctant to admit the reason. "I thought it would make my cats feel better if they heard my voice. There have been studies," she rushed on, "that suggest pets cope better with separation if they can hear their owner's voices."

"Were these scientific studies?" Jim teased her.

"I answered your question," she said somewhat testily.

"Okay, I'm here because the babies seemed a little lonesome so I'm watching some video wallpaper on your TV and giving them a few pats on the head. Did you know that Cheddar likes to play with my fishing pole?"

"Jim, I hope you removed the hook."

"Taylor, dear, do you think me a moron?" Jim was enjoying this.

"Well?"

"What!"

"I'm thinking." Taylor toyed with him.

"Okay, okay." Jim loved playing these games with her. She was getting pretty good at giving back.

"So, really, why should I visit a vortex?"

"I am shocked. Don't you read our spiritual book line?"

"A few of them, but mainly the mystery line keeps me busy. Are you going to explain?"

"Vortexes are said to be energy centers in that some people, supposedly those tuned-in and turned-on, can meditate, or experience altered consciousness, life-changing experiences, past life regression and other New Agey stuff."

"You don't sound like a believer."

"What can I say? The Bermuda Triangle is also a vortex."

"That doesn't sound friendly."

"Definitely not."

"Oh!" Taylor looked at her watch, "I've got to go for dinner. It's served *promptly* at seven and I'm already late."

"What restaurant serves only at seven?"

"Here's a news flash for you. I'm staying at Crystal's."

"You mean to tell me you go out there armed with contracts and lawful threats and she asks you to stay?"

"Perhaps she likes to keep an eye on the opponent."

"Have you gotten anywhere?"

"Only made my first pitch."

"You should have been at the office today." He'd saved the best part for last. "Jessica threw one of her famous fits. I'm afraid most of the Crystal Visions file has been destroyed."

"What! My file?"

"The same. I straightened it the best I could."

"But why?"

"Answer that and we'll all know. Anyway, Jessica stormed out and left for Los Angeles. *Business*, I presume."

"Right, business." Taylor was upset. How dare Jessica go in her office and ravage her things. She was glad she had a backup of that manuscript in case any pages were lost forever.

"Indeed."

"I really have to go now." There was nothing to gain in further discussion of Jessica's behavior. "It's been a long day. I'm starving. And Jim ... "

"Yes, luv?"

"Thanks for cat sitting."

"Just part of the job description." She smiled in spite of herself. Jim could be a soft touch when he let his guard down.

A second before she hung up, Taylor could have sworn she heard something. Was someone listening on the line or had the noise come from outside? She couldn't be sure. It was probably wind. She was too tired to care.

The dining table was set for one. It looked very lonely. The house across the street had warm lighted windows glowing with friendliness. Crystal's house didn't have that same warmth. Taylor sat down and began eating the already cooling soup. It was delicious, even lukewarm: delicate broth with chicken chunks and vegetables topped with tortilla strips. Only those floating above the soup were still crunchy. Taylor made a mental note not to make phone calls right before meals. If Consuela was this good a cook she didn't want to miss a single bite. There was iced water and a bottle of

Riesling next to her place setting. She poured it into the waiting glass and sipped the fruity light wine.

"Did you enjoy your soup?"Consuela asked from the hall.

"It was marvelous. Thank you."

"Do you prefer your chile hot or mild?" she asked.

"Oh, hot."

The main dish was a concoction, almost a stew but served on a plate, of marinated chicken with chiles, onions, tomatillos, and tomatoes. It was similar to fajitas without the tortillas. Two side dishes made Taylor's mouth water—fresh guacamole and green serrano chiles.

"Will Crystal be joining me?"

"Not this evening, ma'am; she had to go out."

"Would you care to join me?"

"No ma'am, it would not be proper." She hustled back in the direction of the kitchen.

The dinner was splendid. Consuela was a talented cook. The seasonings mingled perfectly to produce the distinctive flavor of the southwest. There was a hint of Native American influence as well. Taylor ate past the point of being full. Consuela cleared and presented a flawless flan. Taylor remembered sharing one with Victor a few months ago. It had been a bittersweet moment where she remembered her husband Dave, while seeing the possibilities with someone new. She had felt guilty at the thought that there could actually be someone else in her life, and yet, ecstatic about the prospect.

Taylor carried her dessert plate into the huge kitchen and placed it on the counter next to a triple sink combination. The kitchen was a real piece of work—two islands, one with yet another sink. Taylor guessed that washing up would not be a problem. The other island could be used for food preparation or casual dining. The refrigerator and stove were of restaurant size and quality, and over the sinks, a window served as a pass-through for outdoor dining. The breakfast nook, as large as most dining rooms, protruded from the house in a semicircle with windows all around. A round table with *bancos* made an attractive place to breakfast. The open-ended kitchen became a second living area at the far end.

Here, the room was cozy and offered a built-in entertainment center. Warm wooden cupboard doors covered the entire center so the TV and other electronic components were hidden until needed. Bookcases rose on either side of the doors. Only a few books lined these shelves as though the house was inhabited by nonreaders. Comfortable overstuffed furniture covered in chintz made the room seem welcoming. The feel was another thing entirely. Crystal's house was cool and inhospitable despite the decorator's efforts. There was something almost sinister about it in all its grandeur.

"May I help you?" Consuela startled Taylor.

"Oh! I didn't know anyone was around."

Consuela viewed Taylor as a mother would a disobedient child. Her face was full of reproach.

"I just brought back my dessert plate," Taylor explained, feeling guilty when she shouldn't. "The room was so lovely I couldn't help but admire it."

"I see," Consuela said coldly. "But you would have seen it in the morning at breakfast."

Taylor ignored her mood. "I think I'll do some exploring tomorrow. What would you recommend I see in Sedona?"

"That would be a good idea," Consuela eagerly agreed and Taylor wondered why? "You will, of course, want to see Tlaquepaque. It's a lovely shopping area. The Chapel of the Holy Cross is popular with tourists. The whole area is beautiful. There are the vortexes."

Taylor got the distinct impression that Consuela didn't think much of tourists, but Taylor preferred a more personal exploration of new territory.

"How about hiking?"

"You may hike in Boynton Canyon. The entrance to the Canyon is down the road about a quarter mile. It is clearly marked."

"What about the vortexes?"

"Humph." Consuela was apparently a skeptic too. "You'd have to ask Ms. Visions about that."

"Have you worked for Crystal long?"

"Only a few months."

"Really?"

"Yes, I began working here when Ms. Visions bought the house."

"So, she hasn't lived here all that long."

"No, ma'am." The formal tone had returned.

"Will Crystal be back soon?"

"I wouldn't know ma'am. She keeps her own hours. Sometimes she returns at morning."

"Interesting."

"Yes, ma'am."

Taylor had had enough ma'am-ing for one evening and said good night. She strolled down the main hall toward the entrance. Consuela was bustling about the kitchen so Taylor took a peek in Crystal's study. It was located across the foyer from the dining room and featured a bay window. It was the only room Taylor had seen that could be called tousled. This was a working room. Her desk was mostly unidentifiable since it was covered with stacks of paper, a computer and printer. Taylor hoped it was her manuscript in progress. Deep shelves covered one wall. These were filled to overflowing with books and a small pottery collection. A bar with sink crowded the entrance to a small bath. All in all it was the only room Taylor had seen that indicated someone lived here.

Fearing she was pushing her luck, she left and crossed the hall to the main living room. It, too, was an oddly shaped room extending out from the house in a triangle shape, except for the massive fireplace that flattened the triangle. Windows lined the two long walls. They were undraped. Furniture, more formal here and walnut like the dining room, sat away from the wall of windows. Electrical outlets had been installed on the floor to prevent tripping over cords. Planters full of small cacti stood on either side of the entry columns. The columns were repeated at the fireplace. The cathedral ceiling was much higher than the one in the foyer. It was a room that could contain a very festive party. Taylor imagined an enormous Christmas tree with no-holds-barred decorations. Christmas was only a couple weeks away. It seemed unlikely that Crystal would have a tree. She thought if the author normally decorated, it would have already been done by a professional.

Maybe she could buy her friends gifts here—and her sister Tawna, who now lived in Paris. Yes, she might as well get in some shopping. She had the feeling Crystal would continue to be uncooperative.

It was nearly nine-thirty when she returned to her room. Something about it didn't look right. She was sure she'd left the door to the bathroom open. Maybe Consuela had closed it for some reason. The bed was not turned down, so why would Consuela have been in her room? Taylor concluded that she was very tired and didn't remember. Tomorrow was another day. She'd read that somewhere.

CHAPTER 13

Inasmuch as Crystal did not materialize for breakfast, Taylor elected to do some sightseeing. It was a chilly morning. The temperature hovered around freezing but the sun was glorious in a cloudless sky and the afternoon promised to be near fifty-five. She donned jeans and a black turtleneck topped off with a bulky white sweatshirt that she could remove later if necessary. Mocs seemed the best choice of footwear. These had seen better days, but with the fine red dust that seemed to permeate everything, the older pair would be most suitable. Their thick rubber soles with lugs would be perfect for hiking.

She drove the SUV to the intersection where she had asked for directions yesterday. Sedona was laid out in three distinct areas. West Sedona appeared newer and was built along the highway. Uptown Sedona paralleled beautiful Oak Creek Canyon and boasted the only grid of streets Taylor could find on a map. The remainder of the city bordered the highway to Phoenix but led first to the Village of Oak Creek. Everywhere were ethereal views of high red spires as tall as 2,000 feet sculpted by erosion and time. The views did not come cheap—the median price of homes in the area was around $470,000, even more expensive than Santa Fe.

Nestled under huge Arizona sycamores was the shopping area built in the likeness of Tlaquepaque, Mexico, a village located in Guadalajara which is populated with artisans and their works. The car bumped over the cobblestone entry. Even the parking lot was quiet, a remarkable feat especially with a busy highway close by. Here at the mouth of Oak Creek Canyon was a little bit of Old Mexico. Fountains beneath the towering trees would play in the summer. Graceful arches led from one cloistered courtyard to another, each more lovely than the first. A variety of paving stones and tiles drew her ever inward. White stucco walls climbed to second levels roofed with red clay tiles. Romantic staircases made of painted tiles enticed her upwards. Wrought-iron carriage lamps hung near each doorway. Ivy covered balconies and portals gave the best views of the carefully created reincarnation of the Mexico hamlet. Every nook and cranny had been planned in charming detail. From huge planters to the smallest terra-cotta pot, every shrub and bush had been placed with painstaking precision. In warmer months, flowers would complete the landscaping. The structures, courtyards and even the passageways had been built around the giant sycamores; the planners had worked with the bending, curving white trunks instead of cutting down the beautiful trees to make way.

Luminarias outlined the roofs, walks, fountains and courtyards. At night, it would be magical. It was a tradition that Santa Fe shared; however, they referred to the lights as farolitos. In New Mexico, residents were pretty evenly split as to a preference for the term farolito or luminaria. In northern New Mexico they were called farolitos while the bon fires of Christmas were referred to as luminarias. The southern portion of the state seemed to prefer the reverse. Taylor thought it an odd thing to quarrel over.

The variety of shops was astounding. Works of art by local craftsman were in abundance. Jewelry, clothing, pottery, sculpture, and Native American goods were prominent and intermingled with gift shops, restaurants and bookstores.

She stopped in a gourmet shop and bought her sister several bottles of hot chile sauce and salsa. France didn't offer much in the way of the southwestern foods for her sister who had developed a taste for the spicy. Taylor made arrangements to have it shipped to Paris. The shipping cost more than the items she was sending and it was going via the slow boat. She'd have to send an e-card explaining.

A novelty store window had small bottles of dirt stacked pyramid style several feet high. The accompanying sign alluded to the powers of the vortex dirt captured in each vile. She could not resist this for Jim, even at seven dollars for a small vessel. It would serve him right.

One storefront caught her eye; a metaphysical bookstore. Taylor headed for the tiny shop located on the lower level near the bell tower. Inside, the store was shaped like an inverted T. To her right was a square area filled to capacity with bookshelves. The other side was crammed with cards, crystals, meditation candles, dried herbs and incense. Sandalwood scented the early morning with a light perfume. Directly ahead of her at the back was a counter, the door behind it leading to an office. A desk near the door was covered in paperwork. Behind the counter, a man sat reading.

"A good, but frosty, morning to you." He smiled and pushed reading glasses up onto his head. He was dressed in a brightly striped serape over a white shirt open at the collar. A tanned face smiled through a new beard in friendly welcome. Taylor thought him vaguely familiar.

"What can I help you with?"

"My friend tells me there are vortexes in Sedona." A grin was working along his mouth. He was fighting it. "I know," Taylor continued, embarrassed at her lack of knowledge. "I don't know what I'm talking about but I am interested."

"No problem. How about a vortex for beginners' book?" The smile was aching to escape. "Just kidding. Here's a map of the vortexes in the area. Why not read these handouts we've made up for some rudimentary information. If you want more information I'll always be happy to sell you books." He slid the assortment of fliers into a paper sack.

Taylor looked at the map. "There's one in Boynton Canyon. I'm staying near there."

"That's my favorite. It's electromagnetic."

"Huh?"

"It is both electric and magnetic. The others are one or the other. It's also a fantastic walk into the canyon; great country."

"I see. Thank you." She moved to leave before she mortified herself further.

"A word of warning—not all spirits you meet in a vortex are friendly. Evil spirits exist too."

Was he kidding? She glanced at his face and saw no sign of the teasing face of a few minutes ago.

"Uh, thanks." There was nothing else she could think of to say.

"Happy vortex questing."

Indeed. Taylor wasn't so sure anymore.

When she returned to Crystal's, there was an orange Volkswagen Bug in the drive. It was dusty and pocked with unsightly dents. Taylor could imagine it covered with large brightly colored flower decals as had been popular in the 1970s. The bumper still offered an aging peace symbol. These items could still be found at Northern Sun and other similar businesses. Crystal hadn't mentioned she was expecting guests. But then she hadn't spoken all that many words to her. Taylor let herself in through the door of the three-car garage. She envied the large garage even more than the spacious house. No one seemed to use keys in Sedona, at least not Crystal. She walked past the laundry room, a room larger than her dining room. It was a Pullman style room and contained a washer, dryer, sink and upright freezer along one wall. High quality cabinets and a drying rack on the other wall. What a luxury. Of course, Crystal didn't use it. Consuela did all the real work while the mistress of the house created and communed.

She rounded the right angle of the back hall. When she reached the spiral staircase she heard excited voices.

"Would madam care to join the rest for lunch?" Consuela had seemingly materialized at her side, startling Taylor.

"Please call me Taylor." She recovered her composure. She had been openly listening. "And yes, I would like lunch. Who are the other guests?"

Consuela rolled her eyes heavenward. "Believers."

"What kind of believers?"

"I wouldn't know about such things." Consuela slipped through the entrance of the family room to her kitchen.

The voices were coming from the dining room. Apparently lunch had been moved to a more formal setting in honor of today's guests. Taylor couldn't imagine why after one glimpse of the new people. A heavy woman in a blue jean skirt and crinkled cotton peasant blouse stood twirling, of all things, beads. Her bleached blonde hair hung limply down her back. A floppy hat with a chin strap completed her look.

The man with her, Taylor assumed they were a couple, was as thin as the woman was stout, with silver hair pulled back in a rubber band. His tattered jeans made his companion's outfit look fashionable. Oddly, the new polo shirt he wore seemed the ultimate contrast to the timeworn jeans.

Crystal was turbaned in red, quite becoming as usual, and chatting about the uninitiated. Taylor knew not of what she spoke. She didn't get much chance to think about it because at that moment Crystal saw her standing in the arched door.

"Do come in and meet my friends." Was she serious? She hadn't spoken to her in a pleasant manner since her arrival.

"This is Taylor ... uh, Taylor from my publishing company."

It appeared from Crystal's introduction she had suddenly moved up in the hierarchy of Piñon Publishing, at least momentarily. She was aggravated that Crystal couldn't even remember her last name. What a schmuck.

"She is here to assist with my book." *Assist* with her book? She sure had her nerve. "This is Sky." *Sky?* Taylor shook hands with the man, a man with a slack handshake. And his friend must be what ... sun? Taylor, get a grip, she told herself.

"This is Moonglow." Crystal could actually do the introductions with a straight face.

"Taylor Browning, I'm the mystery editor at Piñon Publishing." She held out her hand.

Moonglow grasped Taylor's hand firmly and smiled warmly. Her round face was friendly and open, like a child's, and her skin crinkled around her eyes in a most attractive starburst. It would be easy to like Moonglow if only Taylor could speak her name without giggling.

Consuela pushed a cart laden with a veritable feast, at least for lunch. It sported an array of fresh fruit, cheeses—Taylor spied some Camembert, her favorite—sandwiches, and left-over tortilla soup from last night. Her mouth watered at the thought. She could eat a couple of bowls of the soup herself. They were seated and Consuela poured a white wine for everyone.

While Consuela served, Crystal talked incessantly about the seminar they would all attend. She barely touched the luscious lunch, but both Sky and Moonglow ate ravenously. The three adjourned with no ado after the last morsel of apple cobbler was eaten, for of all things, a nap. Apparently, from conversation Taylor heard, part of the New Age goings-on would be conducted late into the night. No one clued her in about the festivities.

Taylor returned to her room past the closed door of the bedroom occupied by Sky and Moonglow. She gazed at the beautiful red rocks from her window and sighed. Her assign-ment thus far was both unaccomplished and apparently mis-sion impossible. Would Piñon Publishing disavow all knowl-edge of her actions? She sure hoped her job didn't hinge on getting this one author to cough up a book. It would be eas-ier to get Oscar to cough up a hairball, and more fun, than tangling with Crystal Visions. Obviously, it was going to take more than threats to get the high priestess of print to coop-erate. Taylor would call Jim and ask him to get their attor-ney to take some rudimentary action. They needed this book for their spring catalog. With Dominique gone they needed a frontlist mystery. *Spirit, Mind & Bodies* was it.

CHAPTER 14

Jessica Endicott threw open the inner door to the Piñon Publishing offices. Penny and Candi turned from their conversation at Candi's reception desk to watch in disbelief as the antique mirror fell and crashed in a heap of glass and tin at Jessica's feet. She scuffed at the glass fragments with her canary yellow heels and stopped, face flushed, a few feet from the two women.

"Have that cleaned up," she barked to Candi.

"Don't you have something to do?"Jessica glowered at Penny. "If you are unable to fulfill your duties just say so," she dared the young woman.

Candi rolled her chair back into place at her desk to answer an incoming call. She had ridden out many frays during Preston Endicott's reign. Most of the time they happened upstairs in the administrative offices but it was not uncommon to endure one close at hand. She punched the call through with one red daggered fingernail. Long after the connection was made she pretended to listen and take a message. She would continue to do her eight-to-five thing and hope for another shift in power. Yes, she thought, this too shall pass.

Penny brought her slight body to its full height. Jessica was a head taller thanks to her high heels. Penny repressed the inclination to laugh as she noticed Jessica's cleavage swell to dangerous proportions. So, the lady was a bully. Well, she was accustomed to dealing with bullies. Penny decided to test her secret. First, she'd see what the widow Endicott had to say.

"I've had no trouble with the work thus far," Penny said. "It seems well within my capabilities."

"Being capable is not the same thing as performing," Jessica retorted. "I'm not at all certain that our illustrious senior editor made the best decision when she hired you in my absence. She did not follow my expressed instructions."

"Perhaps the two of you have a communication problem."

"Don't be insubordinate!"

Jessica was a formidable woman and Penny was impressed by her command of a situation she didn't understand. Jessica was a woman who got by any way she could, including making it up as she went.

"That certainly was not my intention," Penny replied."Actually, Mrs. Endicott," Penny said respectfully, "Candi and I were discussing some of last year's records. Perhaps you'd like to step into my office and I'll show you what I've discovered."

"Uh, yes. That would be fine." Jessica made her way upstairs in a skirt much too tight to allow for ease of movement.

Made you blink, Penny thought, and followed her new boss.

Jessica waited impatiently as Penny took her time with the stairs and passed her slowly, carrying a folded expanse of computer sheets several inches thick. She carefully smoothed them on top of her desk, and then leafed through until she found the giveaway page.

"Mrs. Endicott, I moved a long way to take this job—over my parents' objections. You see, I wanted to be independent of them, and their money, and establish my own identity. Now, I've only been here a short time but you seem to have a problem with me. I can't begin to imagine what it might be since you've hardly been in the office long enough to form a realistic opinion about me, so I can only surmise that the problem is not with me."

Jessica slammed the door. "Who do you think you are? You're fired. Do you hear me? Get out."

Before Jessica could reach for the doorknob Penny was around her desk blocking her way.

"I really think you should hear what I have to say about your business, Mrs. Endicott. You will be held responsible and believe me the IRS will hear about your former accountant's creative financing if you choose to fire me."

"What are you talking about? That idiot's already in prison. I didn't own the company while he worked here."

"The IRS might take that under consideration when they receive the news that Piñon Publishing's accounting has been fictionalized, but I think you'll end up paying some hefty fines." She let that sink into Jessica's beautiful red head. "You might also weigh the fact that the audit would seriously cut back on your travel time. If you want to come and go as you please I suggest you start treating me in a much more courteous manner." Penny moved back to the papers on her desk. "Now, if you'd like to see for yourself what I'm referring to."

"That won't be necessary," Jessica snarled and left.

Penny smiled. "Well, Dad, you'd be proud," she whispered. "You always told me that bullies don't bluff well."

*   *   *

Taylor was finishing breakfast, alone. Sky and Moonglow were still behind closed doors and presumably so was Crystal. Consuela had proved herself again as a cook. Taylor had finished a steaming plate of huevos rancheros topped with green chile. If nothing else was gained from the trip, she would go home with a few extra pounds.

She was about to leave when Crystal flounced through the arched entry in an ankle length silk robe of deep purple with matching pajamas. Even at this early hour she was in full makeup. Taylor wondered if she slept in the stuff. She, herself, had only applied a modicum for breakfast because she'd overslept. It had been a difficult night with disturbing dreams that she couldn't quite remember.

"Good morning, Crystal."

"Morning. I see Consuela is taking care of you." She poured a large glass of orange juice at the buffet.

"What? Oh, the breakfast. Yes, she's an excellent cook."

"Not everyone appreciates her menus. Her food tends to be on the spicy side."

"Well, she's found a fan in me." Taylor hesitated to change the subject. This was almost like polite chitchat but she had to make a move soon.

"Crystal, we really have to do some work. I need a timetable for completion for *Spirit, Mind & Bodies*, something concrete. Can we set aside some time today?"

"I have three more chapters ready."

"That's great. When can we expect the remainder?"

"As I've said, creativity cannot be rushed."

"Crystal, you've got to get with the program." Taylor tried for light humor. "It is scheduled for spring release and we need to go to press soon or it will not be ready." One step further. "Jessica Endicott will call in the company's lawyer if we don't get that manuscript pronto." Both barrels. Taylor braced for the explosion she expected.

"You may tell Ms. Endicott ... " Crystal hurled this out and then paused, struggling for control. Her face reddened and Taylor wondered if she should run for her life. Instead of the tongue-lashing she expected, Crystal turned on one golden heel, and marched from the room, effectively ending the conversation. Orange juice spread over the buffet where she had slammed her glass down.

"Hmm," Taylor mumbled to herself.

Somewhere a telephone rang, but not in Crystal's office, perhaps the kitchen. The ring was followed by Consuela's careful footsteps to the dining room. "Telephone for you, ma'am. You can take it in your room."

"Thank you, Consuela."

It was Jim. "Taylor, tried your cell, had to reach you. Stuff is hitting the fan here. Jessica went on another tear—yes, she's back from LA—she and Penny had some kind of *discussion*.

"What's her problem now?"Taylor asked concerned.

"Don't know. I guess she hates it when things don't go her

way. Candi said she blew up at Elise, after whatever happened with Penny, threatened to fire her if she ever caught her doing her nails at work again. Geez, the woman went berserk.

"Anyhow, I called to tell you Eric is coming out to take another photo of Crystal. He should be there some time this morning. It's easier than mucking around with Crystal and having her set it up. It's likely she wouldn't get the photo to us any faster than her manuscript. Anyway, we need one yesterday for the catalog. Eric left at the crack of dawn. I authorized money for a shuttle or to park his car in long-term."

"What does Eric know about photography? I thought he was a graphic artist."

"He studied photography in college along with commercial art. Seems to know what he is talking about. And we're desperate."

"Well, whatever. I'm getting zilch cooperation from her highness. She says you can't rush creativity."

"Nonsense."

"Seriously, Jim, you might as well call our attorney, whoever it is this week. Unless, of course, Jessica has fired the latest one too. At the rate we're going we'll have to start looking in Albuquerque. Santa Fe has a limited number of attorneys."

"Okay. Maybe a short letter to Ms. Crystal will get the ball rolling; crystal ball, of course."

"Very funny. Jim, how are my babies?"

"We've been spending some quality time together. That Cheddar is just about the sweetest cat I've ever known."

"Jim, you didn't like cats until you met Oscar. How could you possibly know?"

"Trust me. I've had relationships with cats, but they weren't made in heaven. Oscar misses you. When I go in the house he tries to look around me. I can only guess that he looking for you."

"Geez, I feel awful. Are they eating?"

"Every time I'm there. Listen, do you have another wall scraper? I seemed to have misplaced the one in the kitchen."

"What do you need one for?" Taylor was puzzled.

"Just doing a little work in your nook; passes the time."

"So, you're not having to scrape cats off the ceiling?"

"Nothing so horrible has occurred."

"There may be another hanging on the peg board in the garage. Feel free to knock yourself out scraping wallpaper."

"I'm not known for overwork."

"Jim?" Taylor hated to ask but she had to know. Jim probably would not tell her if she didn't ask him straight out. "Have any more notes arrived?"

"Negative, Taylor dear. The mad writer seems to have spent himself in your regard."

"What a relief."

"I'll call the attorney right away. Get rough with Crystal if you have to. Virginia's working on another mystery right now in case we don't get Crystal's, but she says it's not nearly as strong as the New Age priestess."

"Virginia finally read Crystal's then? Did she blow a gasket?"

"She read the one in the file, the file that no longer exists. You know Virginia, even if the subject matter was not to her liking she knows a good writer when she reads one."

"Thanks, Jim. I'll watch for Eric. I can't promise Crystal will hold still long enough for him to snap her pic."

"If she prefers our attorney do the snapping, it can be arranged."

"Bye, Jim."

"See you, luv."

There was a small sheaf of manuscript pages on the desk. Taylor dropped into her chair to look at the chapters. Apparently, Crystal left them for her before coming to breakfast. Taylor had a twinge of guilt for coming down so hard on her, but it was momentary. She was still reading when the door bell rang.

Consuela tapped on Taylor's open door. "A Mr. Powers is here to see you, ma'am."

"Thanks, Consuela. I'll be right out."

"He's waiting in the living room."

Eric Powers stood next to the fireplace gazing out the

windows at the desert landscape. The red cliffs were brilliant in the late morning light.

"Eric? Hello, I'm Taylor. We met once briefly at the office." She held out her hand.

"Twice," he said, his eyes crinkling in a very attractive way. "You were there the day I left my resume." He cradled her hand for just a moment.

"Someone who can remember names; how refreshing." Jessica's rude habit intruded into this pleasant meeting.

"I don't follow," Eric said.

"Not to worry. You'll understand soon enough. You're going to fit in real nicely around Piñon Pub." She laughed.

"I only hope I can get one author photo. Jim said I may have my hands full."

"That's the understatement of the year. I'm afraid I compounded the problem today by making intimidating noises."

"You don't look intimidating to me." Eric smiled and Taylor found him disarming.

"I don't think Crystal feels daunted. She left in a huff."

"How do I get to her?"

"Not much chance of that now. Where are you staying?"

"Near the airport."

"Sedona airport?"

"Yes, it's on top of a red rock."

"Isn't everything? Well, I suggest you do some sightseeing while Crystal cools off and try again this afternoon. If I'm not here ask Consuela to introduce you."

"What's on your agenda for now?"

"I'm going to read the new chapters, which Crystal blessed me with and take a hike, literally."

"I think I'll hang around and if Crystal won't see me I'll do as you suggest."

Taylor wished him luck and returned to her room to load her backpack. Santa Fe had many trails in easy reach of the city and Taylor hiked often. Aspen Vista was a favorite during the fall. It was strenuous and took an entire day if she went all the way to the top. Since Boynton Canyon was nearly in Crystal's backyard it seemed the logical first choice.

Maybe hiking would clear her head and help her get some perspective.

CHAPTER 15

Taylor left by the back door. The sun was climbing into late morning and the red cliffs rising nearby glowed in the pure light. She carefully negotiated a massive prickly pear and made her way through scrubby pine. According to her map, she would intersect the Boynton Canyon trail shortly. The entry to the trail was down the road. Hikers had been able to walk directly into the canyon before the housing addition where Crystal lived had blocked the entrance. Now a circuitous route directed hikers around the fabulous houses; wouldn't want to disturb the bondholding class.

The area, considered sacred by the Yavapai Indians, seemed an unlikely site for a contemporary neighborhood. Taylor wondered how the project ever got past the local planning commission.

A few minutes later Taylor found the well-trod path of earth and rocks. It meandered through trees she didn't know by name but appreciated their texture and beauty. Some had elegantly twisted limbs giving each their own character. The sandstone walls appeared terraced by the centuries and green shrubs made dotted lines as if to define each era.

The trail wound its way up and down in lenient curves. It was not a taxing trek of ascent but a lazy excursion into nature at its best. From the trail the houses seemed smaller, though no less imposing, as she looked down at them from along the canyon wall. The adobe colored walls made the best possible complement to the canyon but still seemed far too fresh for this ancient place.

Taylor was pleasantly breathless when she rounded a turn and discovered a large flat rock, a perfect place to sit and take in the scenery. She unbuckled the backpack and sat down on the cool rock. It must have been near freezing before the sun warmed it sufficiently to sit on. She pushed back her hat and took several pictures, working the automatic zoom to bring the rock walls within arm's reach.

With a great deal of resignation she pulled the manuscript pages from the pack and popped a bottle of sparkling water. She was, unfortunately, here to work but it wouldn't take long to read three chapters. The bubbles in the water had a refreshing bite. Taylor let them play out on her tongue. Since she had moved to Santa Fe she had made it a point to drink a lot of water. The humidity level of the arid mountain clime was low and she felt that rehydration was important to good health in the desert. She hoped it was a good skin plumper. Raisin skin didn't have much appeal.

Taylor winced as she finished the chapters. Crystal's manuscript pages were already in excess of three hundred. Piñon Publishing didn't like to publish books much over three hundred fifty pages. It just cost too much. There were lots of drawbacks to long manuscripts, not the least of which was that they tended to lie around in slush piles for longer periods of time. Many people liked to carry books with them and bulky tomes didn't fit in either handbag or briefcase, and certainly not in a pocket. Although there were always some readers who felt that longer somehow meant better, most preferred a medium size book of under three hundred pages.

She shoved the pages back into her pack. After a few moments reflection at the beauty around her, she pulled out the information from the metaphysical store. A small card fell out on the rock. It was made of stiff plastic about the size of a business card. A black square was at one end; the other a color scale.

The card read, "What is your stress level?" The instructions said to place a finger on the black square for several seconds. Taylor pressed her thumb against it and held it tight. No change in color. According to the color scale she was anxious. She placed the card inside her coat sleeve at the cuff and a few moments later, to her delight, the color changed from black to green indicating she was in a peaceful mood. Apparently warm fingers were conclusive evidence of low anxiety. Cool winter days were not favorable to taking tests of this nature. Still, it was fun. Taylor wondered how much warmth it needed to produce blue, the most blissful state. She glanced around quickly and, seeing no one, pushed the card under her clothes against her stomach. This time it changed all the way to blue.

She was absorbed in watching the square go green, then red and finally black, obviously a fascination that could catch on, when a noise from above startled her from this mesmerizing process.

Taylor saw a small boulder hurtling from the craggy cliffs above, causing sprays of pebbles and dirt each time it banged against the canyon wall. She pushed her body against the tree, and covered her head with her hands. It crashed through the limbs of the tree, narrowly missing her head and bumping her right shoulder.

"Hey!" She was on her feet in a split second looking angrily upwards. "What are you trying to do, kill me?" she shouted. No one was there.

"Are you all right?" a man asked.

"Geez, you scared me more than the landslide." Taylor tried to mentally slow her rampaging adrenalin. The man looked familiar. He had changed from serape to a ski jacket but she was certain he was the man from the bookstore.

He kicked at the offending boulder and marveled at its size."You're lucky it missed you. This could have been fatal."

Was it Taylor's imagination or did his voice have just a touch of irony.

"It did hit me," she retorted. "My shoulder will never be the same." She was angry. "Just where were you when this thing was headed straight for my brain?"

"Me?" he said in apparent surprise. "I was hiking out of the canyon. I watched it all from about twenty yards up the trail."

"How do I know that?"

"Surely, you don't think I scrambled down a nearly sheer wall in the few seconds it took for this to fall?"

Taylor had to admit it didn't seem feasible; however, she was in unfamiliar territory and there could be an easier way down. She couldn't see a path anywhere nearby so she did the only thing she could do under the circumstances—apologize.

"I'm sorry. It scared me and I took it out on you."

"What's going on here?" Eric Powers asked, taking in the large man.

"Would you people stop sneaking up on me?" Taylor started again. "I've had about all the surprises I can take for one day," she said. "Eric, this is ... I'm sorry I don't know your name?"

"Samuel Waters." He extended his hand to Eric. "The lady and I met briefly in my bookstore yesterday.

"I see you're already vortex questing," this to Taylor.

"Well, sort of, I like to hike and you were right. The canyon is beautiful. I'm Taylor Browning," she added.

"Well, if you don't need any medical care for that shoulder I'll be on my way. Have to open the store at noon."

"Yes, of course. Again, I'm sorry I jumped to conclusions."

"No problem." He tipped his tan wide-brimmed hat and continued along the trail.

"What happened?" Eric asked.

"This rock," she kicked at it lying at her feet. "This fell and nearly collided with my grey matter. Samuel was on the trail and I all but accused him of pushing it at me. He was really quite nice about my allegations. Look," she pointed at the wall of rock behind her, "he couldn't have thrown it and gotten down to this trail in the time it took to fall. I'm so embarrassed."

"You can't be too careful. Come on, I'll walk you back."

Only a few yards along the path Eric stopped. "Look, Taylor." He parted a few evergreen limbs. "Through these trees is a path. It looks like a pretty easy one."

She hadn't noticed it when she passed by earlier. Several pines hid the entrance. Taylor couldn't see the trail in its entirety but it certainly allowed easy access to the rocks above.

"But, he was on the other side of me on the trail. It couldn't have been him."

"Maybe not, but in all the confusion he could have managed an illusion." Taylor starred at him in trepidation. "Hey, I'm not saying he did it. I'm just saying it's a possibility."

"What reason could he have to hurt me?"

"He probably didn't. I'm only pointing out the possibility."

"You're right, of course. But it likely just fell because it was ready to; Father Time and all that."

"How about I buy you some lunch? It'll take your mind off this. Might even be fun."

Taylor agreed and they returned to change. She stood in front of her bathroom mirror and looked at her shoulder. It smarted with every touch. Her arm worked as expected. Nothing appeared to be broken, just sore. With a groan, she pulled on a red turtleneck and a black wool jacket. A deep crimson scarf probably made some kind of statement but she hoped it would keep her warm.

Once seated in the small sandwich shop Taylor asked, "Were you able to get Crystal's picture?"

"Sure, and while I was at it I took several of Beyoncé."

"No luck, huh?"

"Her housekeeper thought she'd be back later, maybe for dinner. I'll see if I can get one then. I'd like to get back to Santa Fe. The cover proofs should be back any moment and I need to approve them."

Taylor took a deep draw on her iced tea. "Maybe I can smooth over the tension I caused this morning. Her new chapters are very good. Conceivably a compliment could mollify her perspective of me. At least for most authors it would."

"No comment," he said and smirked.

CHAPTER 16

Taylor was awakened a few minutes after midnight by a sound somewhere in the house. She'd fallen asleep while reading a book on her Kindle.

"I guess I should expect things to go bump in the night at a mystery writer's house." At home, Oscar and Cheddar always gave the illusion that someone was listening to her. It surprised her to discover she felt silly talking to herself without them.

She missed them desperately, so turned her thoughts to earlier that evening when Eric had managed to charm Crystal into not one but several poses for his camera. Taylor was in awe of his ability to both profusely apologize for the loss of her former picture and simultaneously lather on the praise for her book—which he hadn't read—and maneuver her into a shot in her office hard at work on her latest runaway bestseller. What a silver-tongued devil. She'd made furious mental notes but didn't know if it would play as well coming from another female. Eric left before dinner and should be half way home by now. She hadn't realized that while he was there she hadn't felt alone. That feeling had crept back right after dinner, compounded by the inadequacy she felt about not having been up to the task of getting Crystal's finished manuscript.

Sleep had almost regained its edge when the noise was repeated.

"Great." She tossed the covers back on the bed, shoved her feet into slippers. "This is a spooky old house considering that it's practically brand new."

The hall was dim. A wall sconce glowed softly lighting the way. She walked straight ahead past the telephone alcove and the powder room, pausing next to the spiral staircase to listen for sounds of life from the other guest room. Nothing. The slapping sound seemed to be coming from the kitchen. If the house had been fitted with shutters she might have suspected that as the culprit, but although this fabulous house had plenty of windows none utilized a shutter.

Taylor had the overwhelming feeling she was the only one in the house. For a moment she thought of her nice warm guest room and yearned to return to its supposed safety. Having read too many mysteries, she liked a smaller house where one could stand in a central location and see into every room. A house like Crystal's would require far too much valuable time checking closets, and it was so big that a person with villainy on his mind could hide where you'd already looked.

This was an irrational and nonproductive thought process, but it allowed her to postpone investigating the sound. It was probably just a red rock mountain lion smacking his lips in anticipation of a tasty meal of ignorant tourist. Likely he would not give her time to explain how much she liked cats.

"Pull yourself together. It's nothing." With this self-admonishment she crept several feet forward until she had could see down the long, softly lit hallway. No one.

The kitchen was equally empty but the clamor was louder. It was coming from the back porch.

"Oh no. I have to go outside!"

A light radiated from beneath the tile covered stove vent making it impossible to see through the windows. All she could see was her reflection looking back at her. If anyone was out there, she would be clearly delineated and completely at his mercy.

"Don't be silly. There's no one out there." A warning flag sprouted in her mind. It reminded her of this afternoon's incident, causing her to doubt her own reassurance.

The breakfast nook with its rounded shape provided no cover because of the many windows that occupied every segment of its five sides. The back door was closed. Taylor reached out tentatively to touch the graceful handle. She felt, more than heard, the next bang as the storm door flapped in the wind.

"Thank goodness," she muttered. "It's only a door." It closed easily and she was about to return to her room by way of a late-night snack, when she noticed the glow a short distance from the house.

"A fire on a night like this?" No one in their right mind would start a fire in such high wind. Taylor grabbed a jacket hanging from a rack near the door and trudged into the night. She would read these guys the riot act on campfires. Okay, so she would determine their location and call a ranger; so much for her fearless woman persona. No one knew better than she how lacking in courage she was.

Ominous clouds swiftly rolled by overhead making night trekking treacherous. Occasional moonbeams gave Taylor some assistance in avoiding the ever present prickly pear. A leg full of sharp needles was the last thing she needed. She clutched at the rough denim jacket in a measly effort to keep warm. She'd had better ideas than a moonlit walk through the desert. Rocks made the going tough and she was about to forget the whole thing when she saw what was happening in the clearing.

In addition to the fire she had seen from Crystal's house, about a dozen people clustered together near a glowing row of red-hot coals. One man was walking across the embers. The others were cheering him on.

"Good grief! What do they think they're doing?" Taylor exclaimed quietly to herself.

A roaring bonfire crackled eerily in the almost windless canyon. The high rocks kept the wind at bay here. Cinders rose and drifted off, fading to black in the cool night. A shovel lay next to the fire and she presumed it had been the instrument of choice for scattering coals. Buckets of water stood nearby should the fire escape its stone boundaries.

The faces of the participants were flushed with excitement at this bizarre affair. Taylor could not tell if it was the flush of reflection or fearful anticipation. The walker completed his short journey and shrieked with apparent delight. The others applauded and hugged him joyously.

Taylor gasped as Crystal came to the head of the line and kicked off her slippers. A quick scan of everyone there told her both Moonglow and Sky were present as well. The remaining people were strangers except for one. It was the second time today she had run across Samuel Waters. He seemed to be turning up everywhere lately. Had he been innocently hiking as he'd claimed? Anyway, what reason could he possibly have to want to hurt her?

She remembered Eric's words: "He probably didn't." For a moment she felt reassured.

But one had only to check their news feed to know there was no end to the violence one person could, and happily would, inflect on another without any apparent motive. Violent crime was in the news every day.

Crystal's eyes were closed. She seemed to be meditating or praying prior to taking the plunge. Taylor watched, squelching the scream that threatened to explode from her. Why didn't someone stop this awful ... what? Initiation? Crystal's right foot settled softly on the coals and she did not yelp with pain. Slowly, deliberately, she walked the coals spread before her. Upon reaching the end of the hot walk, Crystal cried out in celebration. Taylor's own feet were burning in sympathy and she ached to run into the clearing and stop this horror. But these people seemed intent on doing this ritual. Their behavior denoted a spiritual mood and Taylor hesitated to disrupt the ceremony.

Taylor had read about firewalking in one of Piñon Publishing's self-help books. Generally, it was used as a rite of passage pertaining to courage or religious faith, but she had no idea why Crystal and her friends were doing it. If it was a ropes course, she would have thought it a team-building activity. Maybe firewalking fell into that category. But to Taylor it was unsettling and frightening despite the walkers seeming lack of concern.

She felt her intrusion would not be welcomed if she was spotted. Taylor stumbled through the dark back toward the lights of the house. After replacing the jacket, she thought better of a snack, preferring a hot bath to warm her. She was racing through the hall past the spiral staircase to the relative safety of her room when she reconsidered a bath for opportunity. Even a spooky attic couldn't be as scary as what she had just witnessed.

She hurried up the twisting hardwood steps to the storage room Consuela had told her about. Even in the dimly lit hallway she could see the delicate hand-carved railing. No expense had been spared even here. Taylor wondered where Crystal's money came from because she'd published only one book before coming to Piñon Publishing. She must have some other means of support.

The last step was to a landing perhaps five feet square. It overlooked the entrance to the guest bedroom that Sky and Moonglow shared—while not walking on hot coals. The telephone alcove was next to their guest room. Taylor's door was barely discernible through the gloom.

Her entrance was unencumbered by locks. The room was just what Consuela told her, a storage area. The ceiling had skylights that provided enough light to keep someone from stubbing their toe. Taylor was grateful for this because she had no intention of switching on the overhead. She didn't want to call attention to her flagrant snooping. But there was a lamp on a box that she risked turning on. It offered little illumination and many shadows.

Boxes and metal filing cabinets lined both sides of the narrow space. The cabinets were banged and scratched with age. An equally old table was squeezed next to them and loaded with paper boxes—ream size. Taylor could smell the dust. That surprised her because the house was so new. The stuff stored here must have been kept elsewhere and moved here.

Behind the table was a bookcase with its back against the wall. Taylor drew a sharp breath in astonishment. Every book on the shelf was Dominique Boucher's—a complete set. She had wondered about the possibility of a family member since Dominique's cruel murder. It had become more apparent when she and Victor found the old manuscripts in Dominique's house in Taos. They were authored by someone named Dannie Beldon. At the time, they assumed Dominique was writing under a pseudonym since the initials were the same.

Taylor considered what to do. Should she open some boxes and see who had written them or creep back down the stairs and retreat to her room? She had already committed, at the very least, a rude invasion of her hostess' house. On the other hand, she had been sent here as a part of her job and so far had failed miserably at fulfilling her employer's request. Okay, so it was a demand. If she could learn something that might help in this quest she should do it, but Taylor knew from her limited experience in sleuthing that she was a rank beginner and as such would likely be discovered. Of course, that hadn't stopped her before. She opened a box.

It was one of Dominique's manuscripts, yellowed with age. Taylor guessed it was one of the first. It wasn't the stack of paper that was interesting though but the inscription on the first page. She took the single sheet to the lamp and read it.

"To Dannie, with love. Donna." So Dominique had been Donna Beldon! Taylor loved being right. This only encouraged further meddling. She eagerly opened another box in a different stack. It was another manuscript by Dominique. A few boxes down she met with an interesting sight. This manuscript was written by Dannie Beldon.

"Who on earth?" Realization hit like the proverbial bolt. Dannie must be Crystal!

Before she had even a second to digest this tidbit she heard footsteps in the hallway below.

"Oh no," she muttered. Quickly, she turned off the lamp before it gave her away.

She sprinted quietly to the door and opened it a crack.

Crystal, Moonglow and Sky seemed elated after their adventures in the New Age and were chatting excitedly in the hall near the kitchen. Taylor wanted to hear but she didn't dare walk out onto the landing. She would be seen. She wouldn't, however, be seen if she flatten herself on the landing and looked below through the banisters. She crawled through the door and dropped flat. This could be viewed as an indignity but she pushed that out of her mind. No sooner had she settled her supine body for the best possible view than the group began moving her way.

Crystal said, "I have that information upstairs."

Taylor's heart pounded somewhere in her throat as she waited to be uncovered and mortified. Crystal was already at the foot of the stairs. Taylor couldn't force breath in her body. It wouldn't have made it to her brain anyway for all the pounding going on up there. For a moment she considered the possibility that she, in fact, did not have a brain or she wouldn't be in this predicament.

Crystal took two steps. Taylor held her breath.

"Wait a minute," Sky said to Crystal. "Let's pick up on this tomorrow." He cast a lascivious glance at Moonglow. Taylor could not mistake that look even in the dimness.

"Very well. Tomorrow."

Crystal stepped down and said her goodnight. The door closed quickly behind the two grown flower children.

Taylor didn't move until her heart rate returned to something near hysterical, considerably slower than abject terror. She hadn't been concerned with squeaky steps on the way up but she sure was now. She hoped the activities in the other guest room would preclude any interest in a creaking staircase. Taylor hurried lightly down, rushed through the hall to the sanctuary of her room.

"Geez, Jim is right. I've got to stop reading all those mysteries. I'm beginning to think I'm some kind of amateur sleuth."

Taylor sat at the end of her bed and fell backward in fatigue. Something crackled under her head. A slip of white paper had been neatly folded. Taylor sat in the middle of the beautiful southwest comforter, her back to the window, stone cold. She wondered if she had remembered to close the drapes. She read it once more just to be sure it wasn't all a nightmare.

"You can run, but you can't hide." It was a nightmare.

CHAPTER 17

Jim Wells watched the snow falling outside his living room window. Four inches of white sparkling fluff had accumulated in Santa Fe. It covered his patio and rested in rounded heaps across the top of his courtyard wall. He sat in the unlighted room and quietly sipped his scotch, resisting the urge to swallow it in large gulps. Lately, it had been more difficult to control his alcohol intake. The holidays always seemed the worst time of year. He had been estranged from his parents since his art career went bust. His feelings were that tough love didn't work on a grown son with a drinking problem. Once he got through New Year's he'd be fine.

All evening he'd sat and considered whether he wanted to mess with a Christmas tree this year. Last year he'd just said nuts to it, but this year seemed a little different. Taylor had her tree up and decorated before she went to Sedona. Every time he checked on her felines he had to redecorate part of it. Then there were holiday doodads and whimsy throughout her house. He'd asked her why she went to all the trouble for herself.

She answered, "Who's more important than me?"

Well, sure, he supposed that was right; she was stuck in the New Age with a kooky author getting nowhere fast and couldn't even enjoy her own decorations.

It was too late tonight to get a tree. The lots were closed, and he'd weave himself right into a DUI. Maybe he'd look at trees tomorrow. His depressed thinking was interrupted by one of his least favorite things—a ringing telephone. He picked up his cell.

"Yo." He didn't bother with hello.

"Jim? Is that you?"

"Taylor?" He tried to shake the alcoholic haze from this head.

"Jim," she gasped. "He's here."

"Who's there?"

"The guy. You know." Taylor was exasperated and not a little frightened. "The one who writes the notes."

"Taylor, luv, you must be mistaken."

"No Jim. I'm not. I just found another note. Here in my room!"

"What does it say?" She read it to him.

"Jim, it's the same paper; same handwriting. It's him!"

"Okay, calm down. There must be some explanation."

"The explanation is; he's here."

"We don't even know for sure that it was a man. It could be a woman. Whoever it is may mean you no harm."

"How'd he or she get into your room?" Jim slurred his words.

"Crystal leaves all the doors unlocked. Anyone would walk right in. It's a huge house. No one would notice."

"Jim, you're rambling. God, tell me you're not drinking. I need you clearheaded."

"Well, if I'd known you'd be coming to me as a damsel in distress I wouldn't have knocked back the last one."

He was really angry with himself. Now someone he cared about needed him and he couldn't clear the cobwebs. He could hear Taylor sniffing.

"Luv, I'm sorry."

"I'm stuck in the middle of Arizona. I don't even know if they have a police department here. Sedona's such a small town. What do I do?"

"First of all, is your door locked?"

"I don't know."

"Go check. While you're at it check the closet and the bathroom too. Go on. I'll hold."

Carrying her cell with her, she stopped short of opening the closet door. It was one of those louvered things that folded back. Taylor tried to take a deep breath, and slammed the door back. Empty. The bathroom door was ajar and it looked empty, leaving, of course, the tub. Taylor had kept shower curtains pulled back ever since she'd seen *Psycho* in a film class in college. The tub was void of any human as well. She closed the drapes to the big, dark outside and felt better.

"I locked the door and I'm alone in my room."

"Good. Is anyone with you in the house?"

"Yes, Crystal and her two friends are here—in their rooms, I think."

"Taylor, I think you're safe—at least for now. This guy's never done anything to hurt you. Stay in your room until you hear the others out and about in the morning. Call me if anything strange happens. In the meantime, I'm going to call Sanchez and see if he has any advice."

"I tried to get him first, but he wasn't at the station."

That hurt. Jim rationalized it was because after all Sanchez was a detective. He didn't feel much better for it.

"I'll get someone to call him at home. Try to get some sleep."

"Thanks, Jim."

"My pleasure, luv. Call anytime if you need to. I'll check on you in the morning." He hung up and immediately called the Santa Fe police station.

After about ten minutes he finally convinced the rookie this was a real emergency and he promised to call Sanchez at home. Jim hung up in disgust.

The young officer's word was good for a few minutes later a sleepy Sanchez returned his call.

"This better be important, Wells. I just came off a double."

"Look, Sanchez, I think you know I wouldn't call you if it wasn't important." He rushed on not giving him a chance to reply. "Taylor called me not long ago. Couldn't get the twerp at the station to give me your home phone number." He wouldn't mention that Taylor had tried to reach Sanchez first. "It appears that crackpot has followed her to Arizona. She's found another note."

"What! How can that be?"

"Got me, but she's convinced it's the same handwriting. I don't have to tell you that she's frightened."

"Of course not, but I can't figure it. The notes had stopped."

"Guess he can play by his own rules."

"Is she safe?"Sanchez asked.

"I think so. She's staying with an author in Sedona. Right now there are several people in the house with her, but I don't think she feels very secure. The guy *did* get into the house."

"I'll call her."

"Her door is locked and I told her to call me if *anything* happened," Jim said.

"Let's hope that won't be necessary," Sanchez said. "Thanks for calling, Wells." He hung up.

"Jerk." Jim punched his phone to turn it off. Sometimes he hated doing the right thing, but where Taylor was concerned, it had to be done.

Victor Sanchez dialed his superior officer. He hoped he wouldn't get any static about his request.

CHAPTER 18

Taylor awoke to the fearless light of day. She was on the floor, having slept there, deciding she was safer wrapped up in a blanket on the floor than lying on the bed. Her sleep had been fitful with sudden jerks, nightmare falls and wakeful fear. Still fully clothed she listened carefully to the sounds of Consuela bustling about the kitchen. She pulled the note from the trash can near the desk and reread it just to be sure she hadn't hallucinated the whole thing. With unsteady hands Taylor shoved it to the bottom of her rucksack. She might need it later. Evidence. Victor had been understandably upset with her on another occasion when she had unwittingly destroyed evidence. She didn't want that to happen again.

Taylor pushed her tangled hair back from her face. It was time for a bath. No way was she taking a shower—one couldn't hear over the noise of the water. She ran hot water and watched as the bubbles mounded high in pristine foam. A mesquite scented candle sat on the counter next to the sink. Taylor moved the squatty terracotta votive holder to the tub edge and lit the wick. She hoped the fragrance didn't smell of a barbeque.

After a none too relaxing soak, she was still uptight. Taylor dressed in jeans, chambray shirt, and sweater vest.

She appraised her image and declared herself confident even though it was the last thing she felt.

Crystal sat in the dining room with Sky and Moonglow. None of them had bandaged feet so presumably everyone had survived the hot coals without scorching skin. The three hunched over the table studying something with intensity.

"Good morning all," Taylor cried with forced enthusiasm.

"Taylor," Moonglow waved her over. "You're the perfect person for this."

"Oh?" Taylor was a bit wary.

"I read palms for a living."

Scattered around the table were drawings of hands of all shapes and sizes.

"We're using these at the conference," Moonglow explained. "What do you think? Are they self-explanatory?"

Taylor studied the drawings. Under each sketch was a description of the personality belonging to that particular shape. It was fascinating. She compared hers to several and decided the characterization of the hand most similar to hers was fairly accurate; except for the comment about her being haphazard. That couldn't possibly apply.

"How about it—may I take a look at your hand?" Moonglow asked.

"I've had that done recently."

Moonglow appeared surprised.

"Well, then you can test me. See if I come up with the same conclusions." Moonglow was so sweet. Taylor suspected she was a gentle creature and well-adapted for the life she had chosen.

"Sure," Taylor acquiesced. It would help her think of something other than the note.

Moonglow cupped her right hand in her lightly calloused one and moved it gently back and forth. Her face was thoughtful while she deliberated.

"Long life-line ... recent changes in your life?" Moonglow looked to Taylor for confirmation.

"So far, so good."

"Two children?"

"No, try two cats. But I consider them family."

"Okay, close on that one. There may be a third dependent in your future." Moonglow smiled sweetly.

Great, just what she needed was another kitten to further infuriate Oscar.

"This is interesting," Moonglow continued, "perhaps you can enlighten me. There is something red in your future. I also see a circle." Her bushy eyebrows raised in question.

"Oh, that. It's already happened." Taylor told about the mishap, or purposeful push, down the ski slope in Santa Fe.

"Could be a coincidence, but I feel this is yet to occur. You should be careful. I see danger here." Moonglow nodded at her open palm. Her hand closed over Taylor's. "I don't wish to frighten you. It may be nothing, but please don't assume it has already been fulfilled. Be circumspect."

That blew breakfast. Taylor's appetite had been squeezed away by the knot slowly tightening in her stomach. She grabbed a croissant and fled to her room where she snatched a jacket and left the house. No sooner had she settled herself on a bench in the backyard sunshine than Consuela called from the back door. She had a phone call. Please let this be good news.

"Taylor, Victor."

"I am so glad to hear your voice." Taylor felt the weight of a burden carried alone lighten. "I tried to get you last night."

"Wells got hold of me. Listen," he rushed on, "I'm coming to Sedona. I don't like the sound of this."

"That makes two of us. Oh god, Victor, do you think he followed me here?"

"I'm concerned. I don't want to come to the house where you're staying. If he's watching, it's better he doesn't realize I'm there. Could you meet me somewhere?"

"You're here?"

"Just arrived in Phoenix."

Victor was here! Everything would be all right. Taylor nearly collapsed in relief. She'd had no idea the strain this was causing her.

"Victor ... thank you."

"It's nothing. I had a little time off coming to me. Might as well visit a beautiful place like Sedona."

"Why don't we meet at one of the Jeep tour places?"

"Sounds good. We can make like tourists."

Taylor gave him an address and agreed to meet him that afternoon. Her feelings were confused, but her trepidation was greatly reduced.

When Taylor pulled in at the tour office, she took a few minutes to appreciate Victor from a purely aesthetic point of view. He'd always been attired in suits in her encounters with him as a police detective. This was a whole new Victor. His back to her, looking at the high cliffs from the parking lot, she could observe him unnoticed. Neatly creased khaki trousers draped nicely and broke at just the right spot over his Wellington's. His hands were plunged into the deep pockets of a navy squall jacket with collar upturned. Why was it men seemed to deplore gloves so much? He was tall, perhaps six feet and obviously in great shape. Taylor felt a tinge of guilt. She was an unfaithful exerciser. She meant to exercise three times a week but more often than not it was once or twice.

He turned as if he felt her eyes upon him and smiled. It was all for her. Victor had completed the tourist look with a tan fedora. The total effect took her breath away. Be still my heart she thought and opened the car door.

Victor greeted her with a companionable hug, which seemed to warm the very air around them. She hoped he didn't notice the blush her face wore but the twinkle in his eyes told her he did. He knew which buttons to push and just loved doing it.

The tour guide called their names and six people strapped themselves into the back of a Jeep. They rattled out of town and turned onto the roughest looking road Taylor had ever seen. It was graveled but not with nice, neat, small gravel. This looked like partially broken boulders strewn about a narrow swath cut from the side of the mountain that ascended swiftly. It was barely wide enough for a single vehicle.

"I thought you didn't like heights," Victor stated.

Taylor looked gloomily down, straight down, the sheer cliff

where the Jeep's huge, clunky tires rolled within inches of the ragged edge and said, "Believe it or not they told me when I called about this that, yes, we would be climbing in altitude but there were no steep falls."

"Could be this person has a different definition of steep?"

The Jeep continued to climb the precipitous path while the driver chatted amiably about the flora and fauna of the area, frequently driving with one hand while gesturing wildly one way and another. A second Jeep loaded with happy passengers on its way home passed on the mountain side leaving them clinging, on the brink of the world. Taylor gagged on the dust that was fast making a sticky mess of her hair. What a great idea this had been. Victor gave her a reassuring smile with no touch of levity. She bravely smiled back and forced herself to look up instead of down. After a grueling trip at a snail's pace up the face of the mighty red rock, they reached the summit.

Taylor took Victor's hand and stepped out on top of the world. She had been so frightened on the way up that she failed to notice the incredible beauty until this moment. The sun was about to crash into the majestic rocks. The pinnacles reached for the sky rich with the final colors of the day. A purple haze kissed the mesas and hills in a loving glow. Vibrant pinks and corals shrieked between the tall columns of rocks, seeking a way out. A few moments later it was all over and tiny stars claimed their place in the sky.

The way down was just as jolting but somehow didn't seem so scary in the dark. She worked at not remembering the perpendicular walls with the piles of large jagged rocks below. Victor patted her hand lightly as the Jeep's tires found pavement at last.

Back at the tour office Victor suggested they have dinner. Taylor had read about a Mexican place a few blocks down the street and they took her car in the cool evening.

Inside they were seated by a huge window overlooking Oak Creek Canyon with beautiful landscaping highlighted with careful lighting. Unfortunately, it was difficult to walk along the creek because much of the land was privately owned.

Taylor thought it would make a lovely park, much like the one along the Santa Fe River. In daylight the towering rocks would dominate the view behind the canyon. Tonight only lights from houses and luxury resorts could be seen, along with the headlights of an occasional vehicle using the same horrendous road they had just traversed. A few tourists strolled in the desert garden around the restaurant, enjoying the evening air.

"Victor, thank you for coming." She pulled the note from her pocket and handed it to him.

"Looks like the same handwriting," he sighed.

"It is the same person," Taylor said with resignation.

Victor rubbed his chin in frustration. He was thoughtful for several minutes after they had ordered.

"Taylor, let's try something. Think back a couple weeks. Has anything strange happened?"

"Strange!" Taylor sputtered. "What hasn't been strange? Things have been downright weird since ... since the night I found Cheddar."

"Why do you say that?"

"Because that in itself was peculiar. Jim and I went to the Lensic, which we don't do often because it's so much trouble to park. So there I was in that parking garage on the very night this adorable kitten needed a home. I mean, can you believe the serendipity? It was as if there was some master plan that I find him—that he would be there in that garage at precisely the moment I was. I no longer believe in coincidence. What about you?"

Victor had stopped listening to specifics. Instead he stared out the window idly watching a couple return to their car. Taylor had said something crucial and he couldn't quite separate it from the rest.

"Victor? Hello?" Taylor was annoyed at his lack of attention.

"Sorry." He smiled tightly. "Something is bothering me."

"That makes two of us," she bristled.

"What parking garage did you use that night?"

"The one on West San Francisco near the theatre." She was

still mad about his inattention. After all, she was the one in danger here. Shouldn't he at least listen to her?

"A murder was committed in that garage and I'm trying to determine what night you were there. What floor did you park on?"

"I don't know." She thought. "Uh, the second."

"What night was it, exactly?"

An exasperated Taylor pulled her out phone and checked her calendar.

"Let's see, I think that was the day I went to the dentist ... no, no, it was the day of the interview with the Santa Fean ... hmm, maybe ... well, it must have been about ... here." She pointed at the day on her calendar.

"Jim and I went to the Lensic on a whim so it wasn't on my calendar."

"Oh god! Was that the night that woman was killed?" Her body went on alert.

"You're scaring me."

"It's not my intention to frighten, but if you were parked on the second floor it's very likely that you could have seen or heard something."

"The only thing I saw—or heard—was Cheddar hamming it up trying to get me to adopt him."

Their meals arrived steaming hot. She'd ordered veggie fajitas and Victor an enchilada combination platter smothered in green chile. Despite her trepidation, Taylor had wolfed down a considerable amount of salsa while waiting on the main event. She wondered if it was possible to get around it all especially after this new insight. She decided to forego the tortillas and concentrate on the luscious grilled vegetables.

"Guess what?" Taylor teased trying to dispel the somber mood.

Victor munched on an enchilada and acquiesced with a nod.

"Remember when we found those manuscripts in Dominique's house? You know, the ones written by Dannie Beldon." Victor nodded again and chased his food with a Modelo.

"I found manuscripts in Crystal's house by Dannie Beldon and also Donna Beldon. I think the two were sisters. She even has manuscripts by Dominique. You can't get Crystal to admit to having another name, but there you have it."

"Have you been snooping again? You know what happened the last time you did that. You found a body."

Taylor frowned. "It was nothing like that this time. Everyone was out firewalking and I just took a few minutes to look through the storage room."

"You're talking about hot coals?"

Taylor explained the bizarre incident she witnessed. She rather enjoyed Victor's look of disbelief so she described the whole nocturnal escapade in detail as his eyes widened slightly and he at least made an effort to act like he believed her.

When she was finished he asked, "Anything else out of the ordinary?"

"You can lower your eyebrows now. Don't you know this is the center of New Age thinking? They didn't even burn their feet." She gave him a smug look.

"Never mind that now." He dismissed her efforts to aggravate him. "I have to know what you saw in that garage that night—besides the cat."

"Like I said before," infuriated now. "I didn't see anything. For one thing, several of the lights were out and it wasn't possible to see into one corner. I heard a noise and it was the cat."

"Think back. Did you hear or see anything else?"

Taylor tried to remember details since they seemed so important to Victor, but really; he must be mistaken because she hadn't seen anything at all.

"I heard a sound, like a child crying, real low. At first, I expected to find a baby. It was kind of spooky with the lights out because that's where the sound came from. I didn't even have my car door open. I unlocked it first and then went to investigate."

"Go on." Victor encouraged her.

"This is stupid. It's not going to help."

"Let me be the judge. Continue." He added kindly, "Please."

"Okay." Taylor took a bite of her dinner and thought. "I

heard another sound—this was a bit weird—like something sinking down. I don't know, maybe a sack of sand being eased onto the floor. But it had to have been the cat because a few moments later he meowed again and walked from beneath a Cadillac. I picked him up and that was that. I took him home. End of story. See, nothing you can use."

Victor was leaning forward on the table. He didn't want to frighten her anymore but he was convinced she had been on the second floor of that garage perhaps during or right after the murder.

"Taylor," he touched her hand. "The sound you described as a sack of sand being placed on the floor. For a moment, can you remember, did you see anything at all in the gloom of that corner? Any movement? Anything?"

"No. Why are you making such a big deal out of this?"

"Because," he weighed his words carefully, "I believe someone *thinks* you saw something. Something he wants to hide."

Comprehension came to Taylor like a punch to the stomach. Her food suddenly became tasteless and foreign to her palate. She swallowed the flavorless mouthful. It fit nicely with the lump forming in her stomach.

"You mean the killer of that woman?" There, it was out. A simple statement.

Victor remembered the lifeless body of a once lovely young woman. "I'm afraid so."

CHAPTER 19

Taylor pushed her half-eaten dinner away.

"I want to go home. I can't believe this. Victor, there can't be a connection to me and that ... that monster. I remember reading about that murder. I didn't realize it was the same night I was there, let alone the same time. They were married? My god, how could he kill someone he once loved?"

Victor had heard all these questions posed before. He dragged them out every time he was faced with these crimes. There was no way to explain how love turns into something ugly and violent.

"Domestic crimes are on the rise and more and more often they end in death. I can't explain it. I wish I could. I can tell you this woman's ex-husband followed her to several states and despite her attempts to change her looks and hide from him, he always found her. He finally cracked."

"Do you know who he is?"

"His name is Gary Adams. He has a long history of reported assault, stalking, and rape dating back to his college days. No charges were filed at the time and his parents' money was effective in hiding what allegations were made. I suspect the girls were bought off. Later on he married and problems developed with his wife. He took out his anger on her. Got himself fired from his job when the company got wind of it. From there things got a lot worse for his wife."

The restaurant no longer appeared as festive as when they arrived. Taylor looked around the large dining room at the many happy faces. In the far corner next to the crackling fireplace a family celebrated a birthday. A girl of preschool age nearly disappeared in a huge sombrero while the wait staff sang "Happy Birthday." Taylor questioned if she would ever feel that carefree again.

"What does he look like?" Taylor asked.

"Hard to tell; the photo we have is several years old. At the time the picture was taken he had dark blonde hair and brown eyes. Records say he's six feet tall—average build. By now he could look very different—long hair, grey hair, no hair. He could have gained or lost weight. It's doubtful he still looks like the executive type."

"What was her name?" It seemed important that she know.

"The dead woman?"

"Yes."

"Linda Smith Adams."

"Linda." She spoke her name.

"I knew a girl in high school by that name." It was irrelevant she knew."So I'm really in danger?"

"Taylor, I hate to scare you but I'm concerned. There something you should know."

"What?" she asked with reservation.

"I couldn't bring my gun. If I had come on department business I could have gotten a permit, but since I took personal leave it's locked up at home."

Taylor's relief at having Victor here was suddenly squashed. A detective without a gun; this was a fine turn of events.

"It is important you not take any chances," Victor said. "No playing detective. I'm going to stay close by but I'd rather that your author and her friends not know I'm here."

"Okay."

"Is there anything else I should know? Has anyone acted suspiciously at all?"

"Only the boulder that nearly hit me on the hiking trail. Eric thought maybe it was the bookstore owner who pushed it."

"Eric?"

"Eric Powers, the new graphic artist at Piñon Pub working with Jim on covers and other promotional stuff. He was here to take Crystal's photograph and returned to Santa Fe."

"What about this bookstore owner?"

"His name is Samuel ...Waters. He owns the metaphysical bookstore in the Tlaquepaque shopping center. He was one of the participants in the firewalking ceremony."

"Do you think he was responsible for the rockslide?"

"I have no idea. I was too busy getting out of the way. Probably it fell by itself. Sedona has an abundance of rocks."

"I'll check him out. In the meantime please let me know when you go out. I'm texting you my new cell number. SFPD took the lowest bidder on our phone service and now we all have new numbers."

Taylor dropped Victor off at the Jeep tour office where he left his car.

"Try not to worry about this. I'll be around." He pulled her hand from the steering wheel and cradled it in both of his. "We'll find him."

But even Victor had doubts. Gary Adams had eluded authorities for a very long time.

She reluctantly headed for Crystal's house at the far end of town. Sedona had been hailed as the "new Santa Fe" by some travel publications, but unlike Santa Fe, it was difficult to do much walking here. The town was essentially scattered along the intersection of two highways. It required a car for most any excursion. She traveled the dark highway west toward Boynton Canyon.

When she turned onto the residential street, she was taken aback by the lights and commotion clogging the very street she needed to take to Crystal's. Taylor pulled the SUV to the roadside, taking care to keep it out of the ditch. In the next moment she discovered that the emergency vehicles were indeed crowded around Crystal's house and not merely blocking the way.

"Now what!" Taylor wanted to go home. She'd had more than enough. She had failed miserably at her assignment.

They would have to go with another mystery as a lead title because Crystal was not going to produce the manuscript. This ... stalker was here in Arizona and now something had happened to ... Crystal? She hurried toward the chaos.

Taylor couldn't tell which emergency service was being utilized. A fire truck sat in the middle of the street. A police car was parked at the curb, motor running. But it was the ambulance pulling away from the house that disturbed her most. Someone was hurt or sick ... or worse. She sprinted across the yard, sidestepping a prickly pear and stopped short of the front door.

Sky emerged from Crystal's house and hurried away with a police officer. The ambulance roared away, sirens blaring. Crystal was standing in the foyer with another officer. Her normally impeccably made up face was streaked with tears. Several flakes of mascara marred her otherwise luscious skin. The officer said goodbye to Crystal and nodded to Taylor as he left through the front door.

"What happened?"

"Moonglow was attacked right here in my house." Crystal was obviously quite upset and twisted her black silk sash savagely. "Someone beat her brutally in the hall just outside your room. The police think she scared the intruder before he could steal anything. I must start locking the house. My dear, please do lock your bedroom door tonight in view of this ugly occurrence."

Taylor was touched at Crystal's sincerity. Moonglow must be a very good friend. She didn't mention to Crystal that she had been regularly locking her door.

Victor should know about this horrible attack. Her call went straight to voice mail so she texted him the bare essentials.

Taylor wanted to get away from Sedona at least for a day and leafed through several travel brochures. She chose Jerome, a former ghost town, as a place to escape to tomorrow.

Her last thought before sleeping was that Moonglow was attacked outside her room. What if the attacker had been looking for her? It was the stuff of nightmares.

*   *   *

Victor sipped bourbon in the hotel bar. He was far more concerned about Taylor than he had let on. After receiving her text, he wanted her to return to Santa Fe. Tomorrow he'd make the arrangements to take her back. For her protection he needed the home town advantage—and his gun.

CHAPTER 20

The drive to Jerome was pleasant, though Taylor couldn't understand why Arizona had designated it a scenic drive because it was so flat. Personal experience had taught her that only highways escalating vertically with repeated switchbacks and dangerous falling rock were normally designated scenic. She was relieved. Things changed abruptly when she reached the base of Jerome. She shuddered as she saw the way to the small town. It had been built, rather stacked, into the side of Mingus Mountain. The two-lane street ascended steeply in three tight bends—corners nearly impossible to make except at the slowest possible speed.

The brochure said the road was open every day of the year. Taylor was grateful she didn't have to operate a snowplow on this narrow plunging drive. She geared down to second and drove cautiously upward, taking care not to look down. This was a complete impossibility since each curve had a perilously high view. Driving down would be more pleasant because she could cling to the mountain instead of the guard rail as she was doing now.

The town, too, perched precariously on the side of a hill called Cleopatra. She'd ponder the reason for the name at a later time. Views from the mostly Victorian-era miniature city were spectacular. Taylor could see as far as the San Francisco

Peaks near Flagstaff, and the red rock formations she had left a short while ago in Sedona.

Some of the houses in Jerome, once considered a ghost town but now a reviving art community, were brightly painted in shades of hot pink, yellow, green and blue intermixed with more traditional white. Many were still achingly in need of restoration, but those that had already benefitted from the effects of a loving hand dotted the hillside.

The tiny downtown reflected its wild and wooly beginnings as a mining town with frank Western architecture. Tall windows graced straight-up facades with squared tops. The not yet renovated buildings seemed to have multiple personalities with several faded signs announcing what they had been at different times during their more productive years. Taylor parked her car on a one-way street and stepped out on a near vertical incline. From what she'd seen thus far, there were no level streets in Jerome. Likely the residents had bulging calf muscles from walking the steep streets.

Taylor ambled down a side street in the bright sunshine. A narrow, long set of steps marched up the side of a hill. It reminded her of Seattle's stairways up sheer urban climbs. The risers sloped one direction and then another. They had settled over the years, making walking a contest of balance control. In another town it would have acted as an alley but here it was used as a short cut to the street above. Walled and fenced yards hugged the stairs and ragtag trees grew along the edges. In summer it would be nicely shaded. Further down she discovered a ditch that trickled water. It reminded her of the Santa Fe River. It was a deep and, of course, steeply pitched water canal. Another set of steps followed the ditch on a parallel path. Someone's backyard dangerously clutched at bedrock near the ditch, the house only a few yards away.

A young silver tabby meowed welcome as he stretched in a sunbeam on the patio. He meandered, as cats do, over to Taylor and offered his head for petting. An almost overwhelming homesickness hit her as she scratched his downy soft ears. She missed Oscar and Cheddar even more than she knew. The tabby conversed for several minutes, yawned and returned to the sunbeam. Taylor continued her walk.

Hunger was urging her to forage for food. She glanced into an old-time bar. It was original and its wood gleamed from years of rubbing elbows, but the barstools were new and constructed of chrome legs and red plastic seats in glaring contrast to the timeworn establishment. Several tourists laughed beneath the copper colored tin ceiling. A sign hanging over the bar declared: "No Sniveling."

Outside she passed a structure that at one time must have been a service station. An old globe gas pump still sat out front, its hose hanging like the trunk of a tired elephant. The numbers "1910" hung over the door reinforced with bars.

Next door was a closed boutique. It lived up to its former image with garish red doors and windows. It, too, had a sign that explained it had once been a brothel, then award-winning restaurant and now brothel boutique. The brick building resembled a shotgun house and looked no wider than two rooms. The upper story made the building seem even thinner.

She found a quaint cafe. During the summer months it had patio dining available, but today it was crowded inside as locals and a few tourists went in for warmth. Taylor found a table meant for two and settled in with her maps and travel brochures. She ordered hot tea and a chicken salad sandwich and people watched.

A cool draft poured through the cafe when the door opened, and it did frequently in this busy restaurant. Taylor stiffened when she recognized Samuel Waters. She hadn't seen him since the gloomy night she witnessed him and others doing the firewalk. He recognized her and headed her way.

"Ms. Browning." He gallantly removed his Stetson. "I'm glad you had no permanent scare from the incident near the cliff."

"Yes, thank you," she replied. "I am quite all right." She wished the air of bravado she was displaying was real.

"Would you mind if I joined you?" He looked around the crowded cafe. "It appears to be the only seat left in the place." He indicated the chair across from hers.

"Please do," she said and didn't mean a word. They were in a packed restaurant where presumably she was safe from attack. She would, however, keep her food and drink under constant watch. The poison deaths of a few months ago had yet to fade from her memory. Taylor shivered at the recollection.

"Mr. Waters, it seems we are meeting everywhere?" She posed the not so innocent question.

"Please call me Sam," he said good-naturedly. "Everyone does. Are you doing some more sightseeing?" He nodded at the travel pamphlets strewn about the tabletop.

"Yes." Taylor's lunch arrived and the waitress took his order. She called him Sam and shoved his shoulder playfully.

"Who's running the store?" Taylor asked.

"One of my assistants. I have a bookstore here too. In fact, I have four bookstores." That explained why the waitress knew him.

"Where are the other two?" She munched on her sandwich which was delicious.

"Scottsdale and Santa Fe."

Taylor nearly choked on her chicken salad. He had a bookstore in Santa Fe! She wiped at her mouth and took a slow sip of her tea.

"Which bookstore in Santa Fe? I thought I knew them all."

"It's new. I've been there off and on for the last month or two. It's called The Metaphysical Santa Fe. Care to guess what the other stores are called?" He smiled as if the joke was on him. Taylor thought it was.

"I've rented a small property on East Palace several blocks from the Plaza. It includes a courtyard. I've added benches to encourage reading and reflection. Next summer we're adding a small fish pool for ambiance. If it goes, I have an option to buy the place.

Taylor tried to uh-huh in the right places. Not only had he been in Santa Fe recently, but his bookstore was very near where she worked. Her heart raced as his face fell into the right place in her memory. He had been clean shaven when she had attended the psychic fair in Santa Fe. She remembered the manuscript page in his old manual typewriter.

Was he toying with her or was she so paranoid she'd suspect anyone?

Sam's hamburger arrived and he wolfed it down hungrily, washing it down with huge gulps of steaming coffee. Taylor didn't know how people could drink coffee that hot. Perhaps their taste buds were forever burned off. She even iced her hot tea.

"Food's good here, isn't it?" he asked when the silence had drifted on too long.

"Very. I guess you eat here often?"

"Couple times a week." He changed the subject.

"How are you enjoying Arizona?" His skin crinkled around his eyes like a department store Santa revealing years spent in the sun. It was hard to resist his laid-back approach. Taylor wondered if it was a loaded question.

"Except for the close call on the trail it has been lovely." She wasn't going to mention the note left in her room or the attack on Moonglow that might have been intended for her.

"I still haven't made it to a vortex. My walk was cut short after the runaway rock."

"Why don't you try the Airport Vortex? It's close by and you don't have to hike to it." He told her how to find it.

"Well, thanks for sharing your table with me," he said and checked his watch, a fabulous gold pocket watch. "Looks like I should be getting back to work."

"It was my pleasure," Taylor said and almost meant it. She would have if she knew beyond a shadow he was not the stalker. One couldn't help but like Sam Waters.

He dropped five dollars on the table and turned to go.

"By the way, take care walking to the vortex. The path goes along the side of a cliff. You wouldn't want to spoil your vacation."

"Thanks, I'll remember that."

He smiled and replaced his hat, said goodbye to someone named Alice, and left.

Taylor looked at her plate and found most of her sandwich still there. She asked for it to go and paid her check at the door. The terrain back to her car made her calves groan. It had been an almost delightful outing. By the time she reached her car she was huffing.

She collapsed in the driver's seat and headed the car down the only route she knew out of Jerome. Taylor held her breath all the way down.

CHAPTER 21

Taylor called Victor's cell upon returning to Crystal's house. She tapped her foot in exasperation while she waited for an answer.

"Sanchez," he answered.

"Victor," she said.

"Where have you been?" he demanded. "I wanted to take you back to Santa Fe today. I returned your call early this morning and the maid said you went out. She didn't know where."

"I went to Jerome to escape all this for a day. I guess I was out of range of a cell tower. There's no way I could have known what you had planned, now is there?" she said ruffled.

"Okay, no damage done. No damage done?" He waited for a reply.

"Do you mean am I alive and kicking? Yes. But, I ran into our favorite metaphysical bookstore owner again, and guess what?" She paused with intent to vex. Victor certainly seemed to want to take over her life.

"Yes, Taylor?" His patient tone. His *she's acting like a five-year-old tenor*.

"Sam Waters owns a bookstore in Santa Fe and he has been there over the past couple months. I thought he looked familiar when I met him at his bookstore here but there was something different about him. Now I remember. He was at

153

the psychic fair in Santa Fe—selling books. I think he was working on a manuscript in his booth—you know, between customers." She paused to draw a breath. "The reason I didn't recognize him—right away, anyhow—besides the fact that we barely talked, is because he is growing a beard."

Victor whistled softly. "That warrants some checking out."

"Do you think he could be the one?"

"Can't be sure. We'll know more after I make a few calls," Victor said. "I think it's important to get you back to Santa Fe. I've booked us on an afternoon flight back to Albuquerque tomorrow. Can you be ready around eleven in the morning?"

"Okay, but what do I tell Jessica? She'll be fit to be tied if I come home without that manuscript."

"If she gives you any trouble I'll explain some facts of life to her."

"Okay, see you in the morning."

"And Taylor?"

"Yes."

"Please don't take off half-way across the state again. I can't keep an eye on you that way."

"It was only a few miles, but okay. I think I'll pack and take a nap. That should be safe enough."

"I'll be in touch." He hung up.

Taylor frowned at the phone and decided not to let him get to her. He did mean well. She pulled down her suitcase from the high shelf in the closet and removed her clothes from the dresser and closet. After quickly rolling everything tightly, except for tomorrow's change, she placed them expertly in the luggage. She'd traveled since childhood and had found this the best way to pack clothes.

Taylor picked up the telephone again and dialed. It rang twice and Candi announced that she had reached Piñon Publishing. Taylor chatted with the lighthearted receptionist for a few minutes. She could imagine her twirling the phone cord with her long fingers, the bright red artificial nails gleaming. When she had to answer another line, she rang Jim's extension.

"Taylor, luv, what's cooking? Crystal perhaps?"

"Very funny. No, I just wanted to test the temperature at the office. Victor insists I return tomorrow and I won't be bringing the manuscript."

"Geez, Taylor, Jessica has initiated hostilities. You've never seen this office so empty. Virginia took half a billion manuscripts home to edit or so she claimed. Alise is talking about quitting, but I don't think she will, because she'd have to actually work somewhere else. Penny's parents are promising her the world if she'll leave the Wild West and return to their East Coast haven. I don't think she will either. She and Jessica had a discussion—the kind you can hear but not understand, believe me I tried. Since then they have avoided one another except for stabbing looks at each other's back. I feel sorry for Penny. Jessica isn't giving her a chance."

Poor Penny, indeed. Taylor felt jealously again and wished she could like Penny, but she'd be happier with the new office manager on her way back east.

"I can't help it. Crystal's friend was attacked in the house and I think it unlikely that our author will be in the mood to write now."

"When is she in the mood?" Sarcastically.

Taylor changed the subject. "How did the photos Eric took of Crystal turn out?"

"Haven't seen Eric. Course he may have been here while I've been out—which is every single minute I can find an excuse. Guess it doesn't matter if we don't have the manuscript."

"Can you check his office and see if he left the photos there? Taylor asked.

"Sure."

"We'll arrive sometime tomorrow evening. If you can pave the way to Jessica I'd sure appreciate it."

"Ha!" Ha didn't sound promising. "She's taking no prisoners right now. I make no guarantees."

"Jim. How are my babies?"

"I think they've had about enough of me. They keep trying to communicate with me but I just don't speak Cat. Other than missing their mistress guardian they appear to be thriving.

They're almost buds now. You'd never know Oscar once hated Cheddar's guts."

"Thanks. You've been great. See you tomorrow."

"And not a moment too soon, luv."

Taylor felt empty after talking to Jim. She missed him too.

She was too wired for a nap and wanted to get out. It occurred to her she still hadn't been to a vortex. That might be the thing to occupy her and release some tension. Reportedly, one could feel at peace in those surroundings. The Airport Vortex was not far away and Sam had said it was an easy walk. Since it was getting late in the day this was the perfect excursion on her last day in Sedona.

A few minutes later she found the not so well-marked airport exit and eased the car off the road onto a small graveled parking area. She was the only vortex seeker this afternoon.

She walked carefully through brush and prickly pear. There were several undistinguished paths near the parking area. All soon meshed into one that led along the rocks to the vortex. Taylor hesitated and took a moment to get past the vertigo. Part of the trail traversed what looked to her like another dangerous cliff among many in the Sedona area. Obviously, it was heavily trafficked by searchers of the New Age.

"There've been hundreds, if not thousands, of people along here; one foot in front of the other. Don't look down," she admonished herself firmly.

The path felt soft underfoot from the deposits of red dust that collected everywhere. Twice she slipped slightly and drew a sharp breath, wondering whether to turn back. By that time she was closer to the vortex location than her car so she trudged on. If she hadn't been so concerned about the height, or rather the possibility of falling, she could have walked to the vortex in less than a minute.

Taylor immediately relaxed upon reaching the open area that extended off the path. A circle of rocks marked the most energy-intensive portion of the vortex. She stood outside the circle and looked out over the wide valley at other high rock formations to the south. She thought she could identify Bell

Rock in the distance. A light breeze carried the cooling air of the fast approaching evening. It was a magnificent place.

Despite that, something bothered her. The circle of red rocks reminded her of the palm reader's forecast later reiterated by Moonglow who insisted the prophecy had yet to be fulfilled. Taylor dismissed the unpleasant thought and entered the circle.

It surprised her. A distinct buzzing or ringing haunted her ears while a tremendous sense of well-being occupied her thoughts. She sat cross-legged in the dust and closed her eyes to the glorious view and waited for whatever might happen. Her reflection turned to Dave and she found the pain had somehow lessened. Taylor remembered the months of her husband's illness, watching him waste away, and the days and weeks following his death, the horrible emptiness, and the prescription that helped her endure the pain. And then, her employer let her go. It was no longer the fresh, unhealed wound of a short time ago. She couldn't determine if it was this place that gave her serenity or if time had really worked its magic, but she cherished the decline of unspoken anguish.

A sound broke into her thoughts. Taylor looked at her purse. It seemed to have come from inside. She looked in the larger compartment first and found nothing amiss. But in the side pocket she found the malachite crystal in pieces. She held the fragments in her hand wondering if she had dropped or bumped her purse.

The legend the crystal seller told her came hurtling back. *Malachite will shatter to warn of imminent peril.* Now she wondered if it was more than a myth. She thought this was a relatively safe outing, but once again she hadn't told Victor she was leaving. Had she inadvertently put something into motion? Regardless, she needed to get back to Crystal's pronto if only to avoid Victor's annoyance.

Before the significance of her discovery fully soaked in and she could leave, her thoughts were interrupted by the sound of shuffling feet. She turned to face the path and the watchful gaze of Sam Waters.

"What are you doing here?" she demanded. He stood in the

long shadows of late afternoon fully blocking the path to her car. She had no idea if there was another way out over the hill behind her. His appearance, again, set her body and mind on full alert. She pushed herself to her feet and ached to be back in the comparable safety of her car.

"I'm sorry I startled you," Sam said. "I'm writing a book on the vortexes of Sedona—that is why I'm here," he added as if more explanation were needed.

The chilly afternoon closed in about her. She had made a mistake coming here so late—coming here at all. In the presence of this man she was afraid. Gone was the feeling of peace she'd experienced only a few moments ago. Sam Waters blocked her route to the road. There would be no getting around him. In the growing dusk she'd probably fall over the edge of the path even if she were able to pass him.

"Peaceful here, isn't it?" he said as if he hadn't been stalking her.

Taylor's mouth was dry. Once before a minor surgery she'd been given something that made her mouth this parched. But now it was fear.

"Yes, it is peaceful here. I'm glad you told me about it." Maybe she could keep him talking.

"You'll need a light to get back down that path. Do you have one with you?" He didn't seem full of malice but then neither had Donald, and the CPA at Piñon Publishing had killed two people and attempted to murder her.

"Uh, no I don't." She couldn't think how to lie so she went with honesty.

"No problem, I have one." Taylor saw a pleasant smile illuminated by the faint light bleeding away in the western sky. He appeared sincere as he pulled a flashlight from his coat pocket.

Her chest was so tight she feared it would explode beneath her tightly crossed arms. That flash was more than ample for the task of bashing in a skull. Taylor wondered if the hill behind her were climbable? Even if she could make the ascent there was prickly pear everywhere.

"You won't be needing that," a voice broke the void. Sam

turned his back to Taylor and looked in the direction of the sound.

The voice sounded familiar but in this surreal location Taylor could not identify it. She was relieved, however, to find someone else here. Now she could escape Sam Waters.

"Won't be needing what?" Sam asked the figure materializing from the dusty air.

"I'll be taking it," he said.

Taylor still couldn't see the man because Sam stood between them but she could see his shoulders stiffen and once again she felt fear.

Eric Powers stepped away from Sam with flashlight in one hand and a gun in the other.

"Eric, what are you doing here? I thought you'd gone back to Santa Fe."

"I've been around," he said calmly.

"Really," Taylor said. "You don't need the gun. Mr. Waters hasn't hurt me."

"Ms. Browning," Sam said, head turned to look over his shoulder at Taylor. "You never had anything to fear from me."

"Well, sure you would say that but what about Moonglow?"

"Maybe you should ask your friend here. He's the one with the gun." Sam nodded to Eric. "Moonglow's real special to me. I didn't hurt her."

Taylor's relief was short-lived when she realized the gun was pointing at her. Confusion was a momentary prelude to horror.

"Eric, I don't understand," Taylor said. "Why?"

"Oh Taylor, really," his voice filled with hateful sarcasm. "You are so naive. I couldn't let you go on. Not after you saw what I did."

"What are you talking about?" Taylor asked. She had no comprehension.

"That night in the parking garage—while you were fooling with the cat I was slicing up my wife. You looked right at me. You know what you saw."

Taylor drew in a hasty breath.

"If I saw something why haven't I told the police?" She was surprised she could think at all, but words were forming.

"Please, do you think me a moron? You've practically lived with the police." That was true but she couldn't tell them something she didn't know. But Eric didn't know that.

"Honestly, I don't know what you're talking about." Of course, at that point she did. The sound she had heard coming from the corner with the broken lights, the creepy feeling she'd had that evening, it all made sense now. She had been on the floor where Linda Adams had taken her last breath.

"Play dumb, Taylor. It doesn't matter. The time for tying up loose ends is at hand. And, Mr. Waters here will get the blame. You'll note I'm using a gun instead of a knife: different MO. You've set up Sam quite nicely. Thank you, by the way."

Eric was certainly insane. He kept flipping the flash around strobing the night air with its beam. He laughed and the musical sound was replaced by the dark edge of hysteria. He was high on madness and it clouded the entire cliff.

"Here's the scenario. We all walk back along the path but only one of us is going to make it to the other side." Eric laughed at his own private joke. Taylor could not remember ever being so cold. He motioned with the light and Sam moved off ahead of her.

She could hear a lone car pass along the airport road but even if she dared scream they could not hear her and there was so little time for help to intervene. Taylor followed Sam out of the vortex to the cliff trail. For the time being Eric held the light so they could see the way in the lengthening shade. She felt the barrel of the gun touch her back once and she recoiled in fear. In an instant she realized that although she missed Dave terribly she wanted to live.

"That's far enough." Eric ordered them to stop.

The silence was petrifying. She always assumed when someone was killed, it was a loud event. Waiting for him to pull the trigger was eternal.

And then she heard one word, "Move!"

Although she would never be able to convince anyone else, she knew that it was Dave's voice. He had never sounded clearer or more certain. There was only one way to go and that was up. Taylor ran vertically until she crashed through a desert scrub. The smell of her own blood was immediately apparent but she was grateful she could feel the sting of the scratches. She was alive.

Taylor scrambled to her feet and began the arduous task of making her way through the twilight along the hill in the general direction of her car. It was painful going as she was unable to avoid the prickly pear in the deep shadows where she tried to stay out of sight.

A pop sounded from below and Taylor froze. She heard the echo of gunfire throughout the great valley of red rocks. But the turrets of everlasting stone could not stop this bad dream; they could only look on as they had for centuries.

"It's over, Taylor," Eric called to her from below. "Your friend is now lying dead—what's left of him. Let's be done with this. I will make it as painless as possible."

Taylor covered the cry with her hand. Her pounding heart threatened to betray her and she crouched beside a giant prickly to catch her breath. She had to get to the car! Slowly, she inched through the bushes and cacti. She wanted to scream—not just from fright—but the sharp needles cut new slices in her legs with every step.

Eric's madness had turned to anger and he shouted expletives at her. He swung the light erratically over the hill, but its beam could not penetrate the distance separating them. He plunged along the path to intercept her.

Aware that Eric was no longer yelling but crashing along the edge, she ran for her car. The dust and fine pieces of rock made her descent back to the road a precarious one. She no longer cared how much noise she made because speed was much more important. The flash moved below her as if an entity in itself. Eric was a faint silhouette but the pulsing beam of light let her know he was gaining on her.

A gully at the base of the hill caught her foot and twisted it painfully. It cost her a precious second. She forced the foot down again and again as she ran for her life toward the glorious sunset. She could see the orange and yellow colors reflected from the top of the SUV. She could also hear Eric's pursuit and he was only seconds from her. Taylor charged ahead hitting her throbbing foot as she jumped into the parking area from a small mound.

The car was unlocked. She threw herself inside and pushed the locking device. The keys were in her pocket. She hadn't dared to get them out while running for fear of dropping them. But there was no time to find them now either because Eric was slamming down the last incline gun in hand. She heard another pop and pitched across the console. Taylor chanced another look. Eric was barreling straight for the car. This was it. No keys; no escape. She turned on the headlights and looked into the face of a madman. She did the only thing she could—she unlocked the door.

CHAPTER 22

Jim punched in the security code at the office. He'd gotten home before he remembered Taylor asked him to look for Eric's photos of Crystal. They would be in the freelance room that currently housed Eric. He raced up the stairs lit by subtle track lighting hung from the ceiling.

Coming into the building after dark gave him the willies ever since the night Taylor was nearly killed in the basement. He was thankful he didn't have to go down there. In the upper hallway brass sconces illuminated the walls in four places, causing large shadows to fall between the offices.

He hated any place this quiet. Jim always had his TV going for background noise. His thoughts were not good company. He resisted the urge to play music on his phone and instead went about his business.

He darted into the first door on his right. The office was in total darkness. No one left a light on and the drapes were drawn. He flipped on the overhead. Its garish light was almost as unwelcome as the dark. Jim partially covered his eyes while they adjusted. He scanned the room for photos. Nothing lay on the light table except a pair of scissors and some tape.

The small work station next to it was jumbled with glue sticks, clip art books that were no longer used and should be thrown away, rulers, paper clips, rubber bands, and an assortment of paper scraps leftover from cover trimmings done earlier. Jim swept those into the plastic trash can below the table. There he noticed the fishing tackle box and briefcase on the floor. He pushed aside several tubular cardboard containers that stored old art and reached for the box.

He used this type of container for his own art supplies—many artists did—they were cheaper to buy than those especially made for artists. This one was pale green with a few paint smudges on the lid. Jim flipped the fastener and found only paints, brushes, pencils, palette knives and a small bottle of linseed oil.

It had that wonderful odor of creativity Jim remembered from his years as an artist. Art director was a good job but it didn't satisfy his need for expressing his own individuality. The challenge of designing a book he usually never got to read was a different sort of creativity, and he felt, not altogether honest.

But there were no photos of Crystal. He replaced it and reached for the briefcase.

His fingers fumbled on the latches.

"Should have had a drink before I came back here," he mumbled.

Jim could manage nicely through the day without a drink, though many times he'd have one with lunch. Today the opportunity had not presented itself and he was getting shaky. The bottle was the only bad habit he'd kept after leaving his former life as a successful artist. He'd blown his whole career on vices.

"Disappointing failure," his father had called him. His bitterness at himself grew if he didn't tip the glass daily.

The initials on the brief case were not EP; definitely not Eric Powers. But what the heck, he had a nosey streak and no one else at Piñon had those initials either. He pulled it off the pile of yellowing manuscripts. He couldn't figure why Virginia insisted on keeping so many of them. As if they didn't get enough of them every day. They used to line the hall until Jessica took over and decreed they be gone. One could hardly walk through Virginia's office without stumbling over stacks and stacks of boxes and envelopes, all full of manuscripts from hopeful writers. These stored here were published books and he wished Virginia would stop being so retentive and throw them out. He'd personally volunteer to carry the ratty, dog-eared, sticky note mess to the shredder.

The attaché was black leather and obviously a good grade. This time the catches flew up on cue and Jim stared at the neatly organized papers, pen held deftly in its own holder and a notebook carefully flipped to a clean sheet.

"Talk about retentive," he grumbled. Jim wasn't one for neatness, preferring that lived-in look for himself. A manila folder on top looked promising. He opened it and pulled out a handful of 5x7 proofs of Crystal.

"Mission accomplished."

He was about to shove them back into the case when curiosity, hampered only slightly by guilt, spurred him on to investigate further. Eric's Piñon contract was in plain sight and he couldn't quite determine why this made him feel alarm. Eric could have borrowed the case or inherited it from someone. That would easily explain the different initials. Still. Jim glanced over his shoulder at the open door, light pouring into the hall. Quietly he closed the door, turned on the small table light and shut off the overhead. Covert activities called for covert methods.

The stool was old and uncomfortable. There was barely room for his feet beneath the table but he shoved some of the manuscripts aside, watching mournfully as they spilled onto the floor. He placed the case on the top among the glue sticks and paper clips to get a better look. Everything in the case was pretty straightforward: a graphics art magazine, an old newspaper folded neatly in half, a comb, several sketches for Crystal's book, and some credit cards.

"Now why would he need these?" Of course for his trip to Arizona to get the photos. Nothing strange there. But there was. The name on the cards wasn't Eric Powers. At least the scrawl on the back didn't look like it. He couldn't read the name. The signature was almost a straight, dark line, the letters so small to be impossible to differentiate. He flipped the cards. The name read G L Adams. Who was that? Maybe a family member ... or he could have stolen the cards! Jim pulled the notebook out and flipped back through the pages. Several references to the project he was working on for Piñon, some telephone numbers—one looked familiar. It was. It was Taylor's. A stab of jealously caught him off guard.

He dug back through the stack of stuff once more, this time picking up the folded newspaper. It was the front page of the *New Mexican*; nothing out of the ordinary. Taxes going up, water rights, something about the expansion of the ski area, a murder in a downtown parking garage, and a list of upcoming Christmas activities. Jim tried to replace everything as he had found it. He'd worry about the precious manuscripts tomorrow. He needed a drink.

Something nagged at him. Why would Powers have someone else's credit cards? Weirder still, why hadn't he given him the proofs of Crystal? Powers knew he needed them. Where was he anyway? Jim hadn't seen him at all; hadn't even realized he was back. He stared at the initials on the case: GLA. He was making too much of this.

Maybe Taylor knew something about Powers the rest of them didn't. He wanted to talk with her anyway. He replaced the briefcase and quickly doused the light.

From his office he dialed Taylor's number; straight to voicemail. Next he called Crystal's home. The housekeeper was a big help. She told him Taylor was out, didn't know where or when she'd be back.

Jim sat at his desk watching his cell phone shake slightly in his hand. His lamp made a small circle of light on his blotter. Dark shadows danced in the corners and he shuddered. At first he dismissed it as a need for a drink but he knew it was more than that. He didn't take much stock in intuition—maybe he'd never needed to. But it was knocking loudly now.

Jim had known this feeling once before on an afternoon of monsoon rain several months ago. Then, as now, he knew that Taylor was in danger. He remembered that frantic drive down a congested Cerrillos in the hail and rain as he tried to get back to the office only to find her in the clutches of Piñon's murderous CPA. She had needed him then and he was sure she needed him now.

He called Victor Sanchez's house in the hope the man used call forwarding. He didn't. The police station was no help. All they told him was that Sanchez was on personal leave. He just couldn't go home and dismiss this foreboding. Jim checked his watch and turned on his computer.

He pulled up the telephone directory for Sedona. Jim printed a copy of every page that carried hotel or motel listings, there were fourteen, and skipped those for resorts—Sanchez didn't make that kind of money.

He had to find where Sanchez was staying even if he had to call every listing. And he had to find out fast.

It took a precious half hour to locate Sanchez. A sizeable portion of the hotels in Sedona were high-brow, so he concentrated on the few moderate to low-end places. With the seventh call he found him. After ten rings the old-school operator returned and asked to take a message. Jim left a message with the hotel and headed home.

He poured scotch, neat, and swigged it. His trembling hands quieted as he itched for the phone to ring. Jim quickly rehearsed what he would say.

CHAPTER 23

Victor was certain after talking with Jim Wells that Eric Powers was Gary Adams. Adams had finally gotten careless, leaving his briefcase at the publishing office. The man's history indicated he was usually more vigilant. His principal intent was to harm others, mostly women, and he was unconcerned with possible retribution. He was without conscience and although capable of blending into the mainstream with his considerable charm and boyish good looks, he did so only to find new prey. Good looks had put many a victim at ease until it was too late. It worked repeatedly for Ted Bundy.

Victor grabbed the phone and dialed Taylor's cell; no answer. Next he tried Crystal Vision's house.

"*¡Hola!*" Consuela answered Victor's ring. He immediately launched into Spanish to her delight. No, Ms. Browning was not in and she did not know her whereabouts. He listened as Consuela conversed with Crystal in both Spanish and English. When she returned he was told that the mistress of the house had declined to speak with him. He implored the housekeeper to try once more and reminded her that it was possible Taylor Browning could be in danger. Again, Crystal refused to come to the phone. He thanked Consuela and hung up in disgust.

"Unbelievable!" He snatched his coat from the hotel bed and slammed out the door. Taylor had told him she would be packing and now it appeared she was out gallivanting around again. He hoped that was all it was. He headed his rental car towards Boynton Canyon. Perhaps Ms. Visions would be more inclined to talk with him in person. Victor persuaded himself that Taylor was buying some last minute Christmas gifts but his experience told him she was at risk.

"As usual she didn't tell me where she was going," he said angrily.

His apprehension only increased as he drove, pushing the speed limit, to Crystal's estate. What was it that palm reader had told Taylor? He couldn't remember, but he was beginning to believe she had been right in telling Taylor to be careful. If only Taylor would listen to anyone.

Consuela answered the door with a mischievous grin. She graciously invited Victor into the spacious foyer. The house-keeper left to fetch her employer. Long minutes later Victor heard an explosion of excited Spanish coming from down the hall as Consuela jabbered somewhat unflatteringly about Crystal as she half dragged her to where Victor waited. He did his best to look stern by the time they arrived.

"Consuela," Crystal snapped, "just shut up. You know I don't understand Spanish. You only confuse the issue when you get excited this way. Consuela gave Victor a conspiratorial look as she passed him on the way back to her kitchen chores. He had an impulse to hug the lovely woman but resisted. She'd probably just gotten even with Crystal for months of mistreatment.

"I never know what that woman is trying to tell me. What do you want?" Crystal addressed him with a curt nod.

"Perhaps you should learn Spanish," he suggested. "It could be very interesting." She only blinked at him waiting. He introduced himself and explained the stalker situation briefly, hoping it would make her realize the gravity of the predicament.

"As I told Consuela when you called a short while ago, I don't know where Taylor is. We've had some excitement of our own here and maybe she wanted to get away."

"It is very probable that the attack on your friend was a foiled attempt to get at Taylor. There may be a connection."

"She came here knowing someone was following her?" Crystal was outraged.

"Hardly. She had only received notes prior to coming to Arizona. We actually thought she would be safer here."

"Still."

"Ms. Visions," Victor forestalled a diatribe, "I must find her. Has she said anything that might give you a clue as to where she is? Anything at all; something seemingly irrelevant. It could be as simple as shopping or hiking?"

"Mr. Sanchez." Crystal slighted him his title but Victor refused to allow her to provoke him. "I assure you she did not share her plans with me. Now, I must get back to my work." She was gone before he could respond.

If only this was happening in Santa Fe, he'd show her a thing or two, haul her into the station, but here he had no jurisdiction. He swore to himself and was about to leave when Consuela returned.

"*Señor*? Ms. Browning wanted to see vortex." Her pronunciation was so bad that she tried to explain. "Magic place."

"Magic place? Where?"

"*Sí*. Come." She walked through the open double doors of Crystal's office. "She has maps." Consuela raised an eyebrow. She was obviously having some fun at her employer's expense. A stack of vortex maps lay on the corner of the desk left over from a past New Age seminar. Consuela handed one to Victor.

"Is this the closest?" He pointed to the one in Boynton Canyon.

Consuela shook her head and pointed to the airport vortex. "It is easiest."

"*Gracias*. I owe you a dinner out." Consuela smiled at the thought of someone waiting on her.

Victor was on his way back to town in seconds. It was the only thing he had to go on and he would check it out immediately. He was soon on the highway but when he reached the intersection of 89A he knew he'd passed the airport exit. He turned around in a parking lot, hurling gravel behind him.

This time he saw the small sign pointing the way to the airport. Consuela told him he would not have to venture all the way up the narrow, steep road. It didn't take long to spot the two cars parked at the side of the road. The SUV, Taylor's rental, had its headlights on. His body went tense, ready for anything. He resisted the urge to make like the infantry and instead drove slowly past the cars. Around the corner he shut off the motor and parked the car as far off the road as possible. Here the shoulder was nearly nonexistent. He slipped into the twilight.

*   *   *

Taylor felt her chances of survival were slim and none. Eric Powers was certainly insane. He had already shot, and probably killed, Sam. By his own admission, he had murdered his wife. There was no reason to stop now. She made a conscious decision, in the few seconds before he reached the car, she would fight with everything she had. For once in her life she would not be a wimp.

She pulled off her gloves and opened the door slightly, she had to, and to her horror the dome light came on. Quickly she pressed her toe against the sensor behind the door to snuff it. This was a complication she had not thought of but she couldn't risk using her hand; she needed both arms and their cumulative strength. There was no time for plan B.

Taylor braced her free foot against the rise next to the door opening and waited. She forced herself to breathe but it came in gasps. Eric was apparently intent on beating her as he was no longer pointing his gun. But he was running straight for her. She tried to stop the horrible shaking. Too much counted on the next couple of seconds.

When Eric was only a few feet away Taylor dropped her foot to the floor, the light flooding from the car startled him and gave her the edge she needed. She shoved the door against Eric, hitting him full in the chest. She heard the awful thud, the angry curse and metal scraping metal.

171

Eric had the breath knocked from him momentarily. He still held fast to the gun. Taylor could see the glint of the barrel. She figured she had just moments to get the car started and get out of there. She was wrong. Eric was already stumbling to his feet and rushing for her. By this time she existed on adrenalin only. Her body was racked with pain and exhaustion. The one millisecond of indecision cost her. Eric grabbed her and began pulling her back toward the path, toward the vortex and the cliff. She kicked and flailed her arms sometimes landing a blow.

What Victor was seeing in the headlights of Taylor's car was nearly astonishing. A man was dragging a kicking, screaming woman across the uneven desert terrain. He pulled out his cell and called 9-1-1. Years of experience told him to call for reinforcements before rushing into a situation that might be deadly alone. He quickly notified the Sedona police of his location and ran after the couple doing the macabre dance of death. There was no reason to play cat and mouse now.

He hurried up the incline avoiding as many of the cacti as possible. A few moments later he could see enough, even in the lackluster light of the car. A man held Taylor very tightly by her arms. Men always seemed to hurt women in the same locations. It was all a power and control thing with men like this. Taylor was fighting but she was tiring. But, the man must be too. Victor determined his line of defense and took his best shot.

"Adams! Let her go!" he shouted. Adams turned in surprise but did not release Taylor.

"Victor! Thank god." Taylor visibly sagged thinking it was over.

"Let her go," he repeated.

"Who are you?" Adams demanded to know.

"Detective Sanchez. You're under arrest for the murder of your wife."

"Then I have nothing to lose if I toss this one to the rocks." He laughed and Victor recognized the hollow sound of a psychopath. This man wouldn't think twice about killing Taylor.

The only reason he hadn't yet was because his game wasn't over. The game was all important.

*   *   *

Sam Waters came back to life having survived the fall. That idiot with the gun thought he killed him, but Sam knew the terrain. He managed to talk his way to the spot where he knew rock projected from the cliff below the path. A split second before the gun exploded, he jumped. Blessed unconsciousness had relieved his mind of the landing but now he wondered if the woman, Taylor, was still alive. He listened for any sounds. As his mind cleared it became cluttered with more immediate concerns. He heard sounds of struggle above him.

He moved carefully, slowly, along the rock ledge so he could see the trail. What he saw was surreal. Two figures were backlit on the cliff. Particles of sand and dust danced in the misty light in accompaniment to the ghoulish struggle of the couple on the ridge. He recognized the man named Eric Powers and, of course, Taylor Browning fighting for her life. And he thought he heard another voice coming from the direction of the light. He had to do something, but what? He couldn't climb in the dark, probably not even in daylight. No, he'd have to think of something here and now. His hands clinched in anger. One wrapped tightly around a rock at his feet.

Sam could see well enough, because of Taylor's bulky jacket, to know which person to target. Nevertheless, it was risky. Even if he hit Powers he could take Taylor with him. But, if Sam didn't try, Powers would throw her over. No question. Carefully, he aimed at Power's head and lobbed the rock upward. Sam wasn't far below—maybe ten feet—but gravity worked against him. He missed and the stone fell through some brush nearby.

Powers went crazy when he heard the rock land. He shook Taylor wildly and she staggered sideways away from the edge.

"You think you can throw stones at me," he taunted Victor. "Big detective. Where's your gun?"

Taylor took advantage of his inattention. She wrenched free of Power's grasp while his concentration was on Victor. With her right fist tightly balled she swung at his face crashing with all her fury into the hard bone of his skull and the cartilage of his nose. Even in the dying light she could see the blood spurting from his ruined nose. She would forever remember the breaking and crunching sounds as her fist broke his face. Her hand throbbed from the impact and bled where her nails had dug crescent slits into the tender skin of her palm. She'd never hit anyone before. It didn't seem to faze people the in movies but in reality, it hurt like fire blasting through her arm.

Victor sprinted the dozen yards separating them. Powers realized he was bearing down. He raised the gun and fought back the tears flowing from his eyes caused by the pain. Victor dove into the fine red dust and slid into home grabbing Powers' ankles. The gun blasted harmlessly into the twilight as Powers fell to the ground with a heavy thud. In spite of the impact of Victor's body, Powers still held the gun.

Taylor forgot how much her hand hurt and fell to her knees choking on the fine granules swirling in the fallout. Powers thrashed wildly. Victor attempted to hold him while Taylor snatched at the gun and missed.

"Get back," Victor yelled at her. "Get away from here."

Helplessness settled over her as she watched Victor struggle to overpower the killer. Powers only seemed to gain more strength as his anger deepened.

"Run!" Victor shouted.

Still Taylor hesitated. The enraged Powers held the gun firmly. As she watched in horror, he gained enough control to point it at Victor. Victor backed away and he and Powers slowly stood—enemies of unequal power.

Sam realized that Powers didn't know the rock had come from him. He reached about in the darkness until he found another, smoother stone. This time it sailed silently through the darkness into the aura of light and impacted with the soft dust at Power's feet.

Powers immediately swung the gun in Sam's direction. Taylor couldn't believe her eyes. She was positioned perfectly to get at the gun but her hand hurt too much to be very effective. With one hurried step she swept her leg upwards and hit Power's elbow with the top of her shoe. The gun, no longer in hand, hung limply from Power's index finger. As he grappled with it Victor hit him full force knocking the gun into the canyon as both men scrambled for footing along the edge.

Taylor watched the two men battle for position just inches from certain death. Sweat poured from Power's brow even in the cooling evening. He was a man fighting for a worthless life. Victor tried repeatedly to move away from the open air next to the cliff but Power's sheer determination kept the two men stationary, and on the brink.

She backed away thoughts racing. Without taking her eyes away from the men she reached down and picked up the top stone of a cairn someone had built in the vortex. She hurled it at Powers' head, but hit his shoulder.

He crumpled and toppled over Victor as he fell. Taylor threw herself against Powers knocking Victor to safety. She tried to jump back out of the way but Powers seized her leg to stop his fall taking her with him over the cliff. Victor tried in vain to stop her.

Taylor felt the emptiness beneath her and screamed. Many times she had felt this sense of falling and had always awakened to find herself safe in her bed. The intense quiet of disbelief was suddenly broken by someone yelling.

"Hug the wall! Taylor, hug the wall!"

A brief remembered statement, "Not all voices in the vortex are friendly," hung in her mind. She didn't have time to decide. Taylor held out her arms and flailed at the cliff wall. The craggy, hard rocks and scrubs pulled at her nails and scraped her hands. She couldn't quite hold on to any of it and wanted to give up so badly but someone kept yelling at her, making her care.

She stopped falling with a crash she thought would surely

kill her. Her lungs went hot with the impact but she held on desperately to the tiny shrub growing bravely from the face of the rock. Cautiously she felt with her feet and found toeholds. She breathed carefully because something hurt in her side.

Someone whispered, "You're all right now." She knew she was. It was Dave's voice and he was very near.

Victor stood in the dying twilight above looking for her. She knew he couldn't see her. Taylor tried to call out but something between a sob and a moan croaked out of her mouth.

"Taylor, are you all right?" Sam's voice floated to her through the darkness. The sound of his voice seemed only feet away and from above.

With difficulty she managed to tell him she was all right. Of course, she was alive, but all right? At least her arms and legs seemed to be working.

Sam relayed to a relieved Victor that she was alive. "Try to relax," Sam said. "Help is on the way."

Sirens blared above and echoed in the valley. Red and blue lights flashed. The next hours were a blur. Taylor talked to Dave, or the air. She thought she talked with Dave. More lights were positioned above and projected downward. Sam was rescued immediately from the small ridge. After some time a rescue worker rappelled down to her and helped her into some kind of basket. He tightened straps around her and shouted to someone to pull her up. The rescue squad members could not believe she was alive, let alone only slightly injured. She refused to go in the ambulance with Sam Waters. She wanted to go with Victor. She wanted never to go anywhere without him.

"Come on," Victor said his arm cupped gingerly around her waist. "Let's get you to the hospital."

"Hang on; I have to do something." Taylor hobbled slowly away in the direction of the vortex.

"I don't think this is a good idea," Victor said softly.

"I'm not going far. I need just a moment. But, please don't leave."

"I'll be here."

Taylor stopped some distance from the cliff. She stood in the darkness. As the siren moved away; she waited. The air was calm but full of the events that had unfolded. A slight breeze curled around her and she felt its warmth. It smelled of Dave. She remembered his essence all too well. His favorite T-shirt was still in a box in her closet. She took it out when she could stand it no longer and breathed of him. His love touched her face and she wept silent tears. There was an inaudible "Goodbye," as though he had moved past her, through her, and now was moving quickly away. Taylor closed her eyes and it was over. Dave had released her to go on with her life; a life without him. A deep sadness overwhelmed her and a tiny stirring of excitement moved within her soul. He was wishing her well.

She turned to face a worried Victor, struggling with his sensitivity toward her needs and his concern about her physical well-being. Taylor held out her hand to this man, who radiated relief and caring, and walked into her future.

CHAPTER 24

Taylor sat in Victor's car clutching the finished manuscript of *Spirit, Mind & Bodies*. Somehow she wasn't surprised to find that it had been complete all along. Crystal had spitefully held onto her manuscript to the very end—with tragic results. Although she had not been directly responsible for the deaths and attacks, her irresponsibility had added to the devastating finale. She was, indeed, Dominique's sister and said she used the name Crystal Visions for creative purposes—to be judged on her own.

Victor touched her hand gingerly. She ached all over. One rib was taped, her was ankle wrapped in an Ace bandage, her arms were bruised where Eric Powers had gripped them, and she was covered in minor abrasions. The emergency room doctor told her she would be sore for a couple of weeks. She changed positions once more trying to get comfortable. It was no good; there were too many bruises to avoid them all.

Gary Adams, aka Eric Powers, had been found dead in a crumbled, broken heap on the valley floor beneath the airport vortex. Taylor was well aware that she could have been there too if Sam Waters hadn't yelled at her to save herself. His knowledge of the area had given her the chance to live and she would be forever grateful. If it hadn't been for Sam ... well, it was too disturbing to think about.

If only she'd seen the real Eric Powers. Victor had assured

her that it was easy to be fooled. Powers was extremely clever and deceived many. In her dreams last night she had tried to help his ex-wife in the garage but to no avail. History couldn't be changed, even in dreams. Victor told her to celebrate being alive—she was lucky—but her happiness was dampened by the death of a young woman caught in an inequitable legal system. She herself had nearly become another statistic.

*   *   *

The lights of Santa Fe twinkled in the distance as she and Victor neared the end of the drive from Albuquerque. As they arrived in the outskirts of the city, Taylor saw that the farolitos were out. The brown bags with lights inside signaled the Christmas season. Christmas! She'd nearly forgotten. It was in two days. By midnight tonight it would be Christmas Eve. This would be a sparse holiday as far as gifts went, but she was incredibly thankful to be alive.

Victor drove through the east edge of downtown to her house. When he pulled into her drive, Taylor was amazed that her house glowed with its own electric farolitos. Who could have done that? Obviously it had to be Jim, but he was a bah humbug type. It was hard to imagine him doing this. Regardless, the effect was enchanting and welcoming.

Taylor found she couldn't turn the key. Her hand throbbed from the punch she'd thrown. Victor took the key from her and unlocked the door.

Cheddar stood in the foyer waiting expectantly. He "owed" softly in recognition. Taylor dropped her small bag and swooped up the tiny kitten in her arms. One orange foot landed deftly on her arm; he snuggled into her neck.

"Oh, how I've missed you," Taylor cried and hugged the warm, soft bundle close. Victor scratched the tiny orange nose and Cheddar sniffed his finger, but his attention was focused on Taylor.

"Did you leave a light on in the kitchen?" Victor asked.

"No, unless Jim did." For a moment Taylor felt the fear rising again but shook it off. The real threat was over.

"I'll check." Victor walked quietly to the kitchen. He took a quick look and motioned to Taylor to come.

Jim was asleep on the banco in the breakfast nook. His full length was bent because his feet rested on the shelf above. Oscar lay across his chest, meatloaf style. He opened sleepy amber eyes and started purring when he spotted Taylor. Oscar leapt from Jim, waking him in the process. Taylor placed Cheddar on the floor and picked up Oscar for his reunion.

"Hi guys," Jim sat up rubbing his beard. "Guess I dozed off for a minute."

Taylor gazed at Jim and noticed the nook.

"Jim, you papered the walls! What a sweetheart. I can't believe you did it, but it's lovely. Oh, thank you." She rushed to his side to give him a hug. She couldn't mistake the enthusiasm with which he returned the embrace. Her rib hurt.

"You must have been here a lot. You really didn't have to ... I didn't expect ... "

"Oh, luv, it was the babies. They missed you, so I just did a little work while I kept them company. Oscar is a fine foreman kitty and Cheddar, well; he tried really hard to help."

The three spent the next hour drinking tea, even Jim. Victor and Taylor filled him in on the whole story. Victor grudgingly gave Jim credit for revealing Eric Powers as the murderer Gary Adams. Taylor was so proud of him for the effort. Jim shrugged it off.

Alone later, Taylor curled up in her freshly papered breakfast nook for one last cup of tea, decaf this time. Oscar lay along her leg, rumbling happily, and Cheddar curled in her lap. She glanced around at her house in various states of completion. Even with the work still to be done she knew it was home.

She had a great life. No mystery about it.

EPILOGUE

Crystal Vision's book *Spirit, Mind & Bodies* made the spring catalog. Her friend Moonglow recovered. She and Sky returned home to California. Jessica left on yet another trip to New York. Virginia carries on. Penny Lane wonders if she fits in the Southwest even though she feels Jessica is now more firmly in hand. Jim took in an aging tom cat he'd been feeding on the sly. He thinks the tabby deserves a pampered old age. Jim plans to ask Taylor out—no doubt she's under his skin. Victor wants to see Taylor on a regular basis. He can no longer ignore his feelings for her—not after nearly losing her. Taylor makes it a point to always carry malachite with her. She still misses Dave, but she wants to get on with her life, maybe even start dating—if anyone asks her.

Thank you for reading the *Looking Glass Editor*.
If you enjoyed Taylor Browning's editorial sleuthing, please consider telling your friends or posting a short review on Amazon, Goodreads or Litsy. Word of mouth is an author's best friend and is much appreciated.

ABOUT THE AUTHOR

G G Collins once worked for a book publisher, before she walked a reporter's beat. Take this experience; add a mystery, a feline companion and a new cozy mystery series resulted.

Collins has been cat mom to a dozen kitties, all with their own eccentricities. Somehow, they end up as pets in her books. Oscar is the reincarnation of her late Abyssinian cat. The character of Cheddar is inspired by her beloved orange tabby. She also loves and writes about horses.

Book Blog:

https://reluctantmediumatlarge.wordpress.com

News, Views & Reviews Blog:

https://paralleluniverseatlarge.wordpress.com